D0055587

CLEAN

ALSO BY AMY REED

BEAUTIFUL

AMY REED

SIMON PULSE

NEW YORK LONDON TORONTO SYDNEY

SIMON PULSE
An imprint of Simon & Schuster Children's Publishing Division
1230 Avenue of the Americas, New York, NY 10020
First Simon Pulse hardcover edition August 2011
Copyright © 2011 by Amy Reed
For information about special discounts for bulk purchases, please contact
Simon & Schuster Special Sales at 1-866-506-1949
or business@simonandschuster.com.
The Simon & Schuster Speakers Bureau can bring authors to your live event. For
more information or to book an event contact the Simon & Schuster Speakers
Bureau at 1-866-248-3049 or visit our website at www.simonspeakers.com.
Designed by Mike Rosamilia
The text of this book was set in Adobe Garamond Pro.
Manufactured in the United States of America
2 4 6 8 10 9 7 5 3 1
Library of Congress Cataloging-in-Publication Data
Reed, Amy Lynn.
Clean / by Amy Reed. — 1st Simon Pulse hardcover ed.
p. cm.
Summary: A group of teens in a Seattle-area rehabilitation center form
an unlikely friendship as they begin to focus less on their own problems
with drugs and alcohol by reaching out to help a new member, who seems
to have even deeper issues to resolve.
ISBN 978-1-4424-1344-3   ISBN 978-1-4424-1346-7 (eBook)
[1. Rehabilitation—Fiction. 2. Interpersonal relations—Fiction.
3. Drug abuse—Fiction. 4. Alcoholism—Fiction. 5. Anorexia
nervosa—Fiction. 6. Family problems—Fiction.
7. Seattle (Wash.)—Fiction.] I. Title.
PZ7.R2462Cle 2011
[Fic]—dc22
2010026771

For all the brave, beautiful souls
who continue to prove that change is possible

CLEAN

CLEAN

PROLOGUE

KELLY

My skin looks disgusting. Seriously, it's practically green. I have big gray bags under my eyes, my hair is all thin and frizzy, and I'm erupting all over the place with giant greasy zits. I look like a cross between a zombie, a hair ball, and a pepperoni pizza. Have I always looked like this? Was I just too high to notice?

OLIVIA

Did I pack my AP Chemistry book? I can't remember if I packed it. I am not ready for this. I am so not ready.

EVA

This place is a body. The walls are its bones or its skin, or both—an exoskeleton, like a crab has. A crab's shell is meant to keep it safe, to protect it from the world; it is made to keep things out. But this shell is meant to keep us in, to protect the world from us. We are cancerous cells. Quarantined. An epidemic. We are rogue mutations that cannot make contact with the outside world. We're left in here to bump around like science experiments. They watch us pee into cups. They study our movements. One doctor says, "Look, that one's slowing down. There may be hope." Another says, "No. They're all doomed. Let's just watch them burn themselves out."

CHRISTOPHER

Everyone's looking at me weird. They probably just had a secret meeting where they voted on how lame they think I am, and the verdict was "very lame." Add that to the fact that they can all most likely read my mind, and basically I'm doomed.

JASON

Fuck you fuck you fuck you FUCK YOU.

EVA

And the halls are like tongues, fingers, toes, like so many appendages. Dislocated. And these rooms are the lungs—identical, swollen, polluted. This one is the stomach, churning its contents into something unrecognizable.

CHRISTOPHER

That's it. They all got together and compared notes and have unanimously decided to look at me weird.

JASON

If I don't get a cigarette soon, I'm going to fucking kill somebody. We can smoke in here, right? They said we could smoke in here.

KELLY

They took everything, including my astringent. Now how the hell am I supposed to clean my face? Do they really think I'm going to *drink* astringent?

EVA

All these rooms—body parts with mysterious names and functions.

OLIVIA

When was the last time they cleaned this place?

JASON

Fuck this place.

KELLY

I can't sleep, as usual.

My third night in this strange bed and I'm still not used to it. I'm just lying here in these scratchy sheets, listening to this place's weird version of night, where the lights are never fully turned off, where the doors are never fully closed, where there is always at least one person awake and on guard.

Lilana is the assistant counselor with hall duty tonight. I can hear her knitting that hideous thing she calls a sweater, the *click, click, click* of those plastic needles. I can hear the deep, watery wheezes of a fat woman with health problems and a history of smoking whatever she could find. She's what you think of when you think of a drug addict. Not me. Not a middle-class white girl with a nice house and still-married parents.

It's been ten minutes since Lilana checked on me. It'll be five minutes until she checks on me again. All this fuss because the stupid doctor at my intake asked, "Do you ever have thoughts of hurting yourself?" Could any seventeen-year-old honestly say no?

I wonder if the buzzing of fluorescent lightbulbs has ever given people seizures. Or if the clicking of knitting needles has ever driven someone to psychosis. Total silence would be better. Total silence I could get used to. But tonight is different. Lilana's walkie-talkie crackles something about a late-night admit. I hear her shuffle toward my room to check on me one more time. I close my eyes as she pokes her head through my already open doorway. I can smell her signature smell, the combination of cheap perfume and sweat. Then she walks away. The *beep-boop-beep* of the code-locked door to the lobby, to the outside, the door we all came through. The door crashing closed. Then silence. Even the lights seem to shut up.

It is several minutes before I hear the door open and Lilana return. There is another set of footsteps. "I can't believe you're not letting me have my own room," a new voice says, a girl, with a stuck-up anger that sounds rehearsed.

"Olivia, please keep your voice down. People are sleeping, *dear*," Lilana says slowly. The way she says "dear" makes it sound like a threat.

Another door opens and closes. I know the sound of the door to the nurse's office. We all do. I can't hear their voices, but I know Lilana is asking Olivia questions now, doing "the paperwork," scribbling things down on a yellow form. She is telling her the rules, going through her bags, turning out every pocket of every sweater and pair of pants, confiscating mouthwash, breath spray, Wite-Out, facial astringent. She is watching her pee in a cup.

I pretend to be asleep when they come into my room. I've been without a roommate since I got here, and I knew my solitude wouldn't last long. Lilana turns on the overhead light and talks in that kind of fake theatrical whisper that's probably louder than if she just talked in a normal voice. I turn over so I'm facing away from them, so I won't be tempted to open my eyes, so they won't see that I'm awake and then force me into some awkward introduction, with my stinky breath and pillow-creased face. I just try to breathe slowly so it sounds like I'm sleeping.

I hear zippers unzip, drawers open and close. Lilana says, "That's your sink. Bathroom and showers are down the hall. Wake-up's at seven. Someone'll be in here to get you up. That's Kelly sleeping over there. Your roommate. Pretty girl."

Pretty girl. My life's great accomplishment. I wait for Lilana to say more, but that's all there is: pretty girl.

There's silence against a background of fluorescent crackling like some kind of horror movie sound effect. I imagine them staring each other down: Lilana with her always-frown and hand on her hip; this Olivia girl with her snobby attitude, probably another skinny white girl like me who Lilana could crush with her hand.

"Do you need anything?" Lilana says, with a tone that says, *You better say no.*

I hear the swish of long hair across shoulders, a head shaking no.

"All right, then. I'm down the hall if you need me. Try to sleep off whatever you're on. Tomorrow's going to be the longest day of your life."

"I'm not *on* anything," Olivia says.

"Yeah," Lilana says. "And I'm Miss-fucking-America."

"Aren't you going to close the door?" Olivia says.

"Not until your roommate's off suicide watch," Lilana tells her.

I hear her steps diminish as she walks to her perch by the med window, right in the middle of the building where the boys' and girls' halls meet, where, during the evening, when the patients sleep and no doctors or real counselors are around, Lilana is queen of this place.

I lie still, listening for something that will tell me

about my new roommate. I hear clothes rustling. I hear her moving things around, faster than anyone should move at this time of night. She walks over to the permanently locked window by my bed, and I open my eyes just a little to see her profile, shadowed, with only a thin outline of nose and lips illuminated by moonlight. I cannot tell if she is pretty or ugly, if she is sad or scared or angry. Darkness makes everyone look the same.

She turns around, and I shut my eyes tight. She gets into the twin bed between the door and mine. Neither of us moves. I try to time my breath with hers, but she is too erratic— fast, then slow, then holding her breath, like she is testing me. Lilana comes by again, looks in to make sure I haven't killed myself. She walks away, and the new girl and I sigh at the same time. Then our breaths fall into a kind of rhythm. They seem to get louder, gaining in volume with every echo off the white walls and linoleum floor. Everything else is silence. The room is empty except for us, two strangers, close enough to touch, pretending to be sleeping.

CHRISTOPHER

Someone's out in the hall yelling that it's time for breakfast and if we don't come out now we'll lose our activity privileges. I'm like, "Are they serious?" to my roommate, and he just looks at me like, *How dare you talk to me?* and walks out the door without saying anything. So I follow him into the hall, and almost everyone's still in their pajamas, and I feel totally overdressed in my slacks and sweater vest. I want to go back and change, but the big black lady counselor is standing in the middle of the hall with her arms crossed like she's ready to beat up anyone who tries to get by her. So I keep walking with everyone else, and I swear they're all looking at me funny, and I just want to crawl under a rock and die.

I get to the lunchroom, and everyone from Group is already there, sitting together like the strangest assortment of people you've ever seen. "Look," Eva says, pointing at a new skinny girl leaving the food line.

"Go get her," Jason says, so I walk over and ask her to sit with us, and she looks at me like I'm crazy, which I'm used to, so I just grab her arm that's literally as thin as a stick and drag her over to our table.

There are four of us already, and the new girl makes five. We've been waiting for our fifth since Jesse got kicked out on Tuesday for stealing Kelly's underwear. I'm the nerdy guy, Kelly's the pretty girl, Jason's the tough guy, and Eva's the emo/goth girl, like we're some drug addict version of that movie *The Breakfast Club* from the eighties, all sitting together like it's the most natural thing in the world even though anyone who saw us would be thoroughly confused. What happens next I guess you could call a conversation, but it's more like a firing squad, and the new girl is our victim. It goes something like this:

Jason: "How old are you?"

New Girl: "Seventeen."

Jason: "What's your drug of choice?"

New Girl: "What?"

That's when I break in and say, "Your drug of choice. You

know, your favorite. The one that got you in here." And Jason says, "Yeah. Like, mine's alcohol. And Eva's are painkillers and weed. And Christopher's is meth." Then she says, "Really? *This* Christopher?" like she doesn't even know how rude that sounds.

Jason says, "Yeah, this kid's full of surprises," and I say, "Thanks," but of course I don't really mean thanks. I'm just trying to be agreeable. Then he simultaneously slaps me on the back and looks at her like he wants to take her clothes off, and I'm just waiting for Kelly's fangs to come out the way girls do when their turf gets threatened, but instead she tries to be fake nice and just change the subject.

She goes, "Like, mine are cocaine and alcohol. Pretty much anything, really, as long as it gets me high. But vodka and coke got me into the most trouble."

Then Eva says, "Rich-girl drugs," and tears a bite out of her limp piece of bacon.

I say, "Be nice, Eva," even though I know by now it is highly unlikely. That's just the way she is. She's either being quiet and mysterious or she's saying something mean and sharp.

Jason says, "I've known a lot of girls who get freaky when they're on coke." And Kelly says, "Oh, yeah?" And I'm like, "Get a room," and Eva's like, "Jesus, Jason. You're such a fucking pig," and Jason says, "And you're a fucking goth dyke. Why don't you and your fag boyfriend Christopher go run off and write poetry and cut yourselves?"

Ouch.

Eva says, "Fuck you," and Jason says, "You wish," and I say, "What about you, Olivia? What's your drug of choice?" because I want everyone to stop fighting.

Olivia says, "I guess I'm here for diet pills, but I don't have a problem with drugs."

"Yeah, none of us has a problem either," Eva says. "This place is really a health spa for kids who like drugs but don't have problems." I pinch her leg because she's being mean, but she doesn't seem to mind. For some reason, she's never mean to me.

"Aren't you going to eat anything?" I ask Olivia, because all she has is a cup of decaffeinated tea, which is all they let us have because they think caffeine's a drug, even though they let everyone smoke like chimneys.

"I'm not hungry," she says.

"Don't you eat?" Jason says. Then Eva says, "I thought jock meatheads like you were supposed to like skinny girls." Then Jason says, "No, we just don't like fat bitches like you, Eva. I like girls with meat in all the right places, like Kelly here." And he puts his arm around her like he's claimed her, and she looks at him like she's proud to be his. Eva goes back to eating her bacon, and Olivia looks at us like she expects one of us to kill her at any moment. This is only her first day and already she thinks we're animals.

KELLY

This place has its own

mini version of a cafeteria, complete with a couple of old ladies
in hairnets dishing out tasteless gruel from behind a counter.
The food looks like it's been sitting out for days, and there's
always a weird smell like floor wax and soggy vegetables. At the
end of the line is a lady with a giant head and close-together
eyes whose only job seems to be to stand there holding a tray
of mini cartons of 2 percent, saying "Milk, milk, milk" every
time one of us passes by. But she says it like "meeelk" and
she never looks anyone in the eye. She just says "meeelk" and
stares off into space like a zombie.

Then there's the nurse with the tray of little white paper
cups with our names on them, full of our daily legal chemicals

and a couple of horse vitamins that smell like crap. The Gas-Huffer gets antipsychotics. The Pregnant Girl gets prenatals. Eva and the Heroin Addict get something called Suboxone for opiate withdrawal. But basically, all the girls get antidepressants and all the boys get glorified speed for ADHD. The nurse watches us swallow with our Dixie cups of apple juice, and she checks our cheeks and under our tongues to make sure we don't trade later with anyone who has opposite brain chemistry. I've learned a lot about prescription medications since I've been here.

We eat and we bullshit and pick on the skinny new girl. Jason's an asshole and tries to hit on her right in front of me, but she just acts like none of us are good enough for her. Christopher acts like his usual choirboy self, and Eva just eats her greasy three-thousand-calorie breakfast and acts like her usual bitchy self. Sometimes we talk to kids from the other Groups, but we always end up back with each other for some reason, even though in the real world we would probably never acknowledge one another's existence. Except for me and Jason, I guess. We'd be the same on the outside as we are in here.

After breakfast it's one of the day's many smoke breaks and more bullshitting. Gas Man tells some story about how he passed out in a ditch in Alaska in January and almost froze to death. The Compulsive Liar with the expensive baggy pants makes up something about being in a gang, but we all know he comes from a small town by the Snoqualmie ski slopes. Then it's time for community meeting, where we sit in a circle and clap for the new people and introduce ourselves by name, city of origin, and drug of choice.

Kelly.

Seattle.

Cocaine and alcohol.

The Compulsive Liar lists off every drug he's ever heard of. Today he adds ketamine because he heard the Scary Heroin Addict say it yesterday.

Then it's time for the first Group of the day. Fucking Group. It's not even ten in the morning and we're supposed to go into tiny rooms with no windows and get deep with total strangers. We have to look at the cartoon faces on the wall and pick one that describes how we're feeling: angry, bashful, confused, anxious. Then we all take turns pretending to bare our souls.

It's bad enough that all thirty or so of us in this place have been assigned to one of six random counselors whose job it is to fix us, and that we're stuck with four other random kids we don't even know and we're expected to talk to each other like we're the best friends we ever had. But it's worse for us, the unlucky few—me, Olivia, Christopher, Jason, and Eva.

We do not have one of those sad-eyed counselors who did too many mushrooms in the sixties and are always talking about "honoring you" and "empowering you." We do not have one of those wisecracking ex-junkies who has a joke to disarm everyone. We do not have one of those sweet old mothers who beat her addiction to chardonnay, found Jesus, and got her master's in social work when her kids went off to college. No. It's worse.

We have Shirley.

GROUP

SHIRLEY: You must be Olivia.

OLIVIA: Yes.

SHIRLEY: I'm your counselor, Shirley. You've probably heard a little about me.

OLIVIA: No.

SHIRLEY: Well, you will. Have a seat.

EVA: Not there. That's my seat.

OLIVIA: What about this one?

EVA: No, that's where Christopher sits.

OLIVIA: Are you serious?

JASON: You can sit here by me.

SHIRLEY: Don't be a shithead, Jason.

JASON: I was just being polite.

SHIRLEY: Everyone, sit down. Why is it so hard for you to do something as simple as sit in a goddamned chair?

EVA: Because we're drug addicts.

SHIRLEY: Thank you, Eva.

OLIVIA: Shirley, I have a paper for AP English due in two days, and I was wondering if I could skip afternoon Group to work on it. I have the outline and the research done, but I really need time to actually write it, and I was wondering if there's a computer I could use to type it up, because my teacher doesn't allow us to turn in handwritten assignments.

SHIRLEY: Olivia, honey, this is rehab, not study hall. You get one hour a day during free time to work on homework, and that's it. You're supposed to be focusing on your recovery here, not getting into Harvard.

EVA: Amen.

SHIRLEY: Eva, shut it.

OLIVIA: But shouldn't you be supporting healthy behavior? Shouldn't I—

SHIRLEY: Olivia, I'm not so sure it *is* healthy behavior with you. Let's move on.

JASON: Welcome to Group, Olivia.

OLIVIA: Is it always like this?

JASON: This is nothing.

SHIRLEY: Hey. Shut it. I'm talking.

JASON: Sorry.

SHIRLEY: Kelly, let's start with you.

KELLY: Start with me, what?

SHIRLEY: How are you feeling?

KELLY: Fine.

EVA: Bullshit.

JASON: Bullshit.

CHRISTOPHER: Bullshit.

OLIVIA: What?

KELLY: Dammit.

EVA: We all said "bullshit."

KELLY: I forgot.

SHIRLEY: Christopher, would you like to tell Olivia what "F.I.N.E." means?

CHRISTOPHER: "Fucked-up, Insecure, Neurotic, and Emotional."

OLIVIA: I don't understand.

EVA: It's an acronym.

OLIVIA: But why did everyone say "bullshit"?

SHIRLEY: Christopher, why do we say "bullshit" when someone says they feel fine?

CHRISTOPHER: Because it means they're hiding something?

SHIRLEY: Good.

OLIVIA: But what if you really do feel fine?

SHIRLEY: Christopher, care to answer that?

CHRISTOPHER: Um, there's no such feeling as fine?

OLIVIA: Why does she keep calling on Christopher?

JASON: Because he's working on his self-esteem.

SHIRLEY: Good job, Christopher. Let's get back to Kelly, shall we? Kelly, look at all the pictures of faces on the wall. Each one has a feeling word associated with it. There are about forty different emotions to choose from. Pick one that fits.

KELLY: I don't even know what some of those words mean. What is "ambivalent"?

OLIVIA: It means the inability to make a choice. Or feeling two opposite things at the same time.

JASON: Whoa, we got a genius here. How many points is that worth on the SAT?

KELLY: Okay, I feel ambivalent.

SHIRLEY: Explain.

KELLY: What do you mean? I did what you asked.

SHIRLEY: What are the two conflicting feelings?

KELLY: I don't have two conflicting feelings.

SHIRLEY: You just said you feel ambivalent.

OLIVIA: This is ridiculous.

EVA: Just do what she says and no one gets hurt.

KELLY: Uh, well, I guess I'm pissed off.

SHIRLEY: At what?

KELLY: At being in here.

SHIRLEY: And?

KELLY: And, uh, I don't know. I guess . . . scared.

SHIRLEY: Scared of what?

KELLY: I don't know.

SHIRLEY: Yes, you do, Kelly.

CHRISTOPHER: We're all scared.

JASON: I'm not.

EVA: Fuck you, Jason.

SHIRLEY: What are you scared of, Kelly?

KELLY: That this is a waste of time. That nothing's going to change. That everything is going to be exactly the same when I get out.

SHIRLEY: Good.

CHRISTOPHER: Yeah, you did really good.

KELLY: Thanks.

SHIRLEY: But I'm not quite sure you understand the definition of "ambivalent."

KELLY

It's movie night tonight, so we're all sitting or lying in the community room in various configurations around our pillows. Rumor has it that they used to allow blankets until someone was caught giving some guy a hand job beneath the sheets. There are now strict rules that everyone must be at least two feet away from the person next to them, so now hand jobs can only be accomplished via telekinesis.

Olivia's over there with her perfect posture like this is the first time she's ever sat on the floor. She's probably fantasizing about all the homework she could be doing right now, or she's writing the rough drafts of all our rehab assignments in her head. I bet she wet her pants in excitement when she found out they give us homework in here, too. Instead of history and math and science, we get these really long writing assignments where we're supposed to pour our souls out and prove how fucked up we are and how everything we do is wrong and stupid.

I just don't get it. I consider myself a pretty smart person—I mean, I got mostly B's all this year even though I was completely wasted the whole time—but I just don't understand the point of all this forced introspection. It's like they think constantly talking about depressing shit will somehow make you less depressed. Either that or they're obsessed with suffering and they get off on listening to everybody's sad stories. That must be it—they get paid all this money to supposedly make us sane when actually *they're* the psychos.

I can make a list a mile long about all of the stupid things I've done when I've been high or drunk, all the ways I've been hurt and all the ways I've hurt other people. Just thinking about it makes me want to get high, and I haven't even gotten into the details. How is that supposed to help me? How is feeling like a failure supposed to help me? The way I see it, they should invent some pill that just makes you forget whatever you want, some pill that makes you numb and functional like the one in that book *Brave New World*. If we had something like that, we wouldn't need any of the drugs and alcohol that got us in here.

But instead they're making us sit on the floor and watch the movie where Sandra Bullock goes to rehab. All the movies they show us have something to do with addiction, and the ending is always the same: The hero either chooses recovery or dies. My first night here they showed a made-for-TV movie about some high school jock in the eighties on steroids. Really? Steroids? Did they run out of movies about real drugs to show? Most everyone fell asleep, and I just sat there in the dark, hungover and shaking from the night before, strung out from the line I snorted before my parents drove me over here, paranoid and miserable and wanting to die, convinced that these people have no idea what they're doing and there's no way in hell they can help me.

Surprisingly, this Sandra Bullock movie isn't too bad. For one, it's a real movie with real actors, not some bullshit Lifetime crap. Not that I'm a fan of Sandra Bullock or anything, but I like how her character doesn't take any shit. The movie's not going to win any Oscars, but it's entertaining enough that I can lie here and try to forget where I am for a couple of hours. Except someone always has something stupid to say. When Sandra Bullock crashes her car when she's drunk, someone says, "Hey, Kelly, is that you?" And everyone laughs, and I say "Very funny" like I don't care, but it really does hurt my feelings. And then when the gay German guy comes on, Compulsive Liar says, "Oh, look, it's Christopher," even though no one actually knows if he's gay, and he's definitely not German, but everyone laughs again and Christopher says absolutely nothing. I can see him in the corner looking straight at the TV in the front of the room, not moving, probably not even breathing, trying to pretend like he didn't hear anything. And I want to go over there and slap him. I want to tell him to stick up for himself for fuck's sake. But he'd probably just nod and look down at the ground and say something Christian like, "Oh, they're just having fun. They don't mean it. It doesn't bother me," when inside I know he's unraveling. How could he not?

Eva says, "Shut up, you fucking Nazi." As annoying as she is, she's pretty fearless when it comes to speaking her mind, which is more than I can say for myself. Tonight's AC, the Ponytail Guy, says, "Eva, that's enough," even though he's always trying to act all sensitive, so shouldn't he be on her side and sticking up for the maybe-gay kid? Eva says, "Why didn't you say that to the homophobe?" So Ponytail says to the Compulsive Liar, "You, too. There will be no hateful language in here." And that's that. Everyone goes back to watching the movie. I look over at Christopher and we make eye contact for a second, and there's this weird look of surprise on his face. Then he looks away, and it's back to Sandra Bullock like nothing happened.

I look over at Jason, and no surprise—he's looking at me. I guess if I have anything in common with anyone in here, it's probably him, though I'm not really sure what that would be. It's just that some people look like they have things in common. And we look like that. We are the kind of people who look like they belong together, even though I couldn't really give you a good reason why. As soon as I saw him, that little buzzer in my stomach went off that means we'll hook up. Then he hit on me, then I flirted back, and now I guess he's my boyfriend. But I don't know. I guess I was hoping things would be different here. Like maybe I wouldn't have to get a boyfriend the second I got here. Maybe I'd actually get a chance to start over like people say. But maybe that kind of thing doesn't really happen. Maybe I'm stupid for thinking this would be a place I don't have to be who I've always been, somewhere I can be somebody new.

I keep thinking about the lady who took my evaluation test, when she looked me in the eye and said, "Honey, don't you want a break?" And all of a sudden my throat closed up and my eyes started stinging and I felt like crying even though I haven't cried in forever, and I had no idea where it came from. It was the strangest feeling, like it hurt and felt good at the same time, like I was more exhausted than I've ever been, but I also felt like I could run a marathon.

I don't know what any of this means. All I know is I feel crazy, like I want to cry and laugh and scream at the same time. I wonder if anybody else feels this way, if anyone in here is as scared as I am. Are they as sad and angry and confused and ashamed? Is that even possible? Is it even possible for one building to hold all that pain?

PERSONAL ESSAY

JASON

What do you want, Shirley? Should we delve into our childhoods so we can realize how awful our parents are? Do you want us to blame everything on them? That seems pretty lazy, if you ask me. Because everybody has fucked-up families, even the normal kids, even the ones who aren't in here. Everyone's parents are either divorced or abusive or don't give a shit. There's no magic math equation that makes us addicts, nothing that separates us from everyone else. We just are what we are. We're just fuckups. There's nothing special about my life, no clues to explain why I ended up in here and not on the honor roll or the varsity football team.

OLIVIA

The thing you need to know about me is that my family's perfect. My grandfather had a high position in the State Department, and my father is following in his footsteps. There's been talk lately about him running for Senate, but I try not to pay attention. His world is not my world. I live in the kids' world, where we're supposed to be perfect and not make any noise. My older brother is a junior at Princeton, fourth generation, bound for Harvard Law, etc. My younger brother is a violin prodigy. Me, I'm my own brand of perfect, I guess. The kind that has to work a little harder than everyone else.

CHRISTOPHER

I don't know where to start. There's nothing particularly interesting about my life. I mean, look at me. I'm dressed in clothes picked out by my mom from the Sears online catalog. I have these old-fashioned glasses and this ugly mop haircut and these stupid brown shoes. Every time I look in the mirror I expect to see someone else, but it's always this pale, squinty-eyed geek who looks like he hasn't gone through puberty yet.

KELLY

I'm pretty sure I know what the point of this assignment is. And don't get me wrong—I think it's a great idea. Just not for me. It makes sense for everyone else to think about their childhoods and parents and stuff, because maybe if they realize they have no control over any of it, then they won't feel so bad about the way they turned out. I mean, kids like Christopher are pretty much doomed to be weird. And Eva with her dead mom, and Olivia and Jason with their pressure to be a certain way—kids shouldn't have that much stress.

EVA

She was the girl with the pigtails. She was the girl with the smile and the laugh like seashells, with the magical powers possessed only by perfect children. The mom in the PTA. The dad who'd take her to Mariners games on the weekends. Rosebushes. A vegetable garden full of nutrition. Three square meals a day made by soft, loving hands.

These memories are shades of pastel, smoky and warm, like drifting off to sleep, like a velvet painting of heaven. They live in a box strangled by chains. To keep them safe. To keep them from the dark that took their place.

JASON

My family's not that bad, really. It's not like I was raised in the ghetto and my dad was in prison and my mom was a crack whore. My dad is an ex–Navy SEAL with, like, a million medals. He owns his own contracting company and makes a shitload of money. My mom makes fancy Jell-O molds and volunteers as a tutor for poor kids. I should be fine. I should be on my way to a great future. So your theory is wrong, Shirley. Nothing made me the way I am. Nothing but me.

EVA

Do you remember? Do you remember the world before the dark? Do you remember the world with mothers and fathers and a stillness that did not feel like death?

OLIVIA

My mother's her own brand of perfect, not brilliant like the men in the family, but regal, I guess because she comes from old money. I don't know that she's ever had a real job. I don't even know what she majored in in college, just that she "met" my father there, even though their parents knew each other and had been trying to hook them up for years; kind of like an arranged marriage, though no one would ever call it that. They were a match made in heaven: Old Money + Old Power = World Domination. It makes sense that their offspring would be required to follow in their footsteps.

CHRISTOPHER

I haven't done crazy things like everyone else in here. I haven't been arrested. I've never been to a party (unless you count church functions). I've never even been to downtown Seattle. It seems like everyone in here is pretty used to getting in trouble, or at least pissing off their parents, but I've never even been grounded before. How embarrassing is that? It's like I don't even deserve to call myself a teenager. My mom still treats me the same as when I was five. She still calls me her "little angel." Doesn't it just make you want to throw up?

KELLY

I think the idea is that if we realize we're not completely to blame, then maybe we'll start believing there's some good left in us after all, and maybe that will make us want to get sober. I mean, nobody just becomes a drug addict for no reason, right? Nobody just decides they're going to be totally lame and lose control and get bad grades and make their parents hate them. I get it, but it's just not going to work for me. All it does is make me feel worse, because now it's just that much more obvious that there's no excuse for why I turned out the way I did. No one ever abused me. No one in my family is an alcoholic. Nothing traumatic ever happened to me. The truth is, my parents are the nicest people in the world and I keep breaking their hearts for no reason.

CHRISTOPHER

This could very well be
the first Sunday of my life that I'm not at church. Even
with chicken pox or the flu or a fever of 103, my mom has
always dragged me with her—as much as she can drag with
her limited mobility. And I guess it should feel liberating
to be away from her, like I'm finally free or something.
But the thing is, I like rules. They make me feel safe. The
predictability of my boring life makes everything make
sense. I guess that makes me a freak, but I'm okay with that.
You get to a certain point and you just realize there's no use
in trying to pretend you're normal.

But now I'm here and I'm surrounded by drug addicts and
criminals, and I'm the kid who doesn't fit in because, among a

million other things like the fact that I'm homeschooled, I'm also the weirdo who'd rather be in church or at home with my mom. Instead of listening to a pastor preaching the word of God, we're listening to a doctor lecture about the synapses and receptors in the addict's diseased brain, and Olivia's taking notes like this is some kind of class, like we're getting graded on how good a patient we are, and everyone else looks like they're going to fall asleep. If my mom were here, she'd be furious at them for filling my brain with such scientific nonsense. She'd start wailing her fire and brimstone, and then it'd be time to take her home and make her a snack. Once she was fed, she'd be ready for a nap, and then everything would be okay and we could go back to normal.

But Mom's at church and I am here, which is probably the farthest you can get from church, except for maybe hell, but I don't plan on going there anytime soon. But who knows? I'm not doing so well so far, am I? The counselors promised that there would be time for God on Sundays because supposedly this is a spiritual program, even though I haven't heard anyone mention Jesus since I got here, except to take His name in vain. They told my mom that leaving the facility, just for an hour once a week to go to church, would hurt my recovery and was "against medical advice," which in their language means "sin." They said, "Do you want your son to get better?"

and of course she knew she couldn't say no, not with all those people looking. What kind of mother would take her kid out of rehab? So she let them have me, and now this is supposed to be my church. Instead of stained-glass windows and framed pictures of Jesus, we've got construction paper self-portraits lining the walls, next to dusty posters that say ONE DAY AT A TIME and KEEP IT SIMPLE and—my favorite—DENIAL IS NOT A RIVER IN EGYPT, whatever that's supposed to mean.

Maybe Olivia has the right idea. Maybe I should be taking notes like a good student, like this is a school assignment. Maybe it's not about being good or bad, but just how hard you study, how well you do your homework, and how many questions you answer correctly. Could it be as simple as that? Maybe I don't need to get down on my knees and pray for healing and for the Lord to take these demons out of me. Maybe I don't need to beg to be cleansed of my sin. That's not how they do things here, and quite frankly, I was getting tired of it anyway. The doctor says my sin is a disease, and I have to admit that sounds like a great alternative to what I'm used to.

The doctor pops in once in a while to give a lecture and meet with us for five minutes to check on our meds. That's about as far as the interaction goes. I can't even remember his name, but apparently he's the one running this place. I have so many questions, but I'm too afraid to ask Shirley and I never get a chance to ask him. Maybe there are some questions I'm just going to have to figure out on my own.

This is what I want to know: What's the difference between a sin and a disease? If a disease isn't the same as a sin, does that mean there's not supposed to be any shame? Is there no shame in being sick? Is this disease from the Devil, or is it just a matter of chemical reactions in my brain like the doctor's talking about? Does that mean it's not my fault? And if it's not my fault, then who's to blame? If it's not my fault, then how should I be punished?

I know this is a lot of questions, but I can't help it. I just need someone to tell me how I'm supposed to feel, because I honestly have no idea.

DRUG & ALCOHOL HISTORY QUESTIONNAIRE

QUESTION #1:

How old were you when you first used or drank?

Tell the story, and how you felt.

JASON

I guess I was, like, nine or something and my dad had some of his old navy friends over. He never let me come in the den when his friends were over, so of course that's exactly where I wanted to be. I'd hide behind something and watch them until they kicked me out. And it was fascinating, you know, all their dirty jokes and cursing. It was the only time

I ever heard my dad laugh at something other than me or my mom.

OLIVIA

I've never been drunk. I've never done *real* drugs. I'm not that type of person. Do you think they can kick me out for not being enough of a drug addict?

EVA

The girl was halfway between a child and a woman. Summer left her broken and without a mother. Ninth grade arrived in another part of town, where there was no boyfriend, where there were no friends, where there was nothing at all familiar, and she had no idea there were so many different kinds of lonely. But she does not want your pity. She just wants you to understand what can happen when you're a million kinds of lonely all at once, when you find yourself among identical strangers you do not want to get to know. Do you realize how easy it is to decide to try something new, how easy it is to close your eyes and spin around and start walking toward the first thing you see? She saw people across the street from school that did not look like the others. They were smoking and they were laughing and they had something new to show her.

KELLY

The first time I drank was with Chris Henderson. He was seventeen and I was thirteen. He lived down the street. He wasn't my boyfriend or anything, but I'd go to his house after school sometimes and we'd make out. We did that a few times and then I'd go home before his parents got home from work. But this one time, his parents were out of town and he gave me a big glass of vodka and orange juice.

CHRISTOPHER

The first drug I did was cocaine. I was fifteen. It wasn't even a year ago. That and meth are the only drugs I've ever tried. I've never even tasted alcohol.

KELLY

The drink tasted awful, but I wanted to impress him so I drank the whole thing really fast. Then we were making out and I realized I was drunk at the same time I realized he was taking off my pants. And, I don't know. I guess at that moment I just sort of knew that the two things go together: sex and alcohol, alcohol and sex.

EVA

She smoked pot with them at lunch that day. She was afraid

she wasn't doing it right, but no one seemed to mind. Their smiles were easier than most people's, and there was something safe about sitting in a circle in the park with all those misfits, something that didn't judge, that didn't require, that didn't disappoint. They didn't ask anything of her, but they gave her smiles and smoke and a place in their circle, and that's exactly what she needed.

CHRISTOPHER

I was with my neighbor Todd. He's the only person I've done drugs with. No one else I know does drugs. I don't think any of them have even smoked a cigarette before. They already think I'm weird enough, but they'd be horrified if they knew what I've been doing. The story my mom came up with is that I'm missing church because I have mono. Even Pastor Tom agreed to keep the secret, and he's, like, a *pastor*, and I'm pretty sure it's part of his job to tell the truth.

JASON

They were watching the game, and my dad saw me and said, "Come here, you little pussy." So I walked over even though I was sure he was going to kick my ass. But instead he gave me a beer and said, "Drink this. It'll put hair on your chest." And everyone laughed, and I was like, I'm gonna show these assholes what a man I am. So I downed the whole thing, like *chug, chug, chug,* and everyone was cheering and clapping and my dad goes, "That's my little man," and he let me watch the rest of the game with them.

OLIVIA

My mother, Janice, decided that fourteen was too old for baby fat so she got her doctor to write me a prescription for diet pills. He's the kind of doctor who can charge his rich clients insane amounts of money because he'll write them prescriptions for anything they want. Janice's medicine cabinet is proof of that.

CHRISTOPHER

Todd and I used to play together when we were kids, but I wouldn't say he's my friend. Actually, if I went to his public school, I'd probably be one of the kids he beats up. He's that kind of guy. But for some reason he started talking to me last year. His house is on the route I walk to church for youth group twice a week, and one day there weren't any other kids around to see him being nice to me, so we started talking. Then we started hanging out a little, but always in secret. He'd climb up the tree outside my window and knock on the window like, "Hey, Chris, are you decent?"

even though he knows I hate being called Chris. Then he'd laugh and jump through the window without even waiting for me to say anything, and my mom never even knew he was there.

EVA

The truth is, it felt good. The truth is, it was exactly what she needed—getting high and laughing a little, not having to think about all of the things that would make her sad, not having to think about the million stupid things that would fill her head and remind her not to smile.

KELLY

The alcohol felt good and it made me not care that I was losing my virginity to this guy I knew didn't care about me. It made me okay with that. It made me okay with everything.

JASON

I was nine, so I guess I was pretty little and didn't have a tolerance or anything, so that one beer really fucked me up. I remember sitting in the den thinking all the navy guys in that room had probably killed somebody, and there they were yelling at the big-screen TV in my house, and what a fucking honor that was, you know?

OLIVIA

My mother handed me two bottles of pills one day and said, "Take two of these every morning. More if you need it. Take the other ones when you need to sleep. Tell me when you need a refill." And that was that. I didn't know what to expect. I didn't realize the pills would actually feel good. I just took them because I didn't want her looking at me the way she does when she's disappointed. I didn't want to overhear her telling my dad how much I embarrassed her.

KELLY

After he was done, he told me to leave because his friends were coming over. I remember how it hurt to walk home. My parents were out somewhere with my sisters, so I went in their liquor cabinet and made my own vodka and orange juice. I wanted to keep the feeling going, because I knew if I didn't, I would think about what I'd just done with Chris Henderson.

CHRISTOPHER

At first Todd would come over with cocaine, but then he started bringing meth instead because he said it was cheaper and lasted longer. I know what people say about meth being a white-trash drug, but really, who am I kidding? We have a broken lawn mower and a plastic pink flamingo in our front yard and my mom hasn't had a job in years. We're not exactly classy. So Todd and I would just sit around and get high, which was weird because, one, I was getting high, and two, I'd never hung out with anyone like him. The only people I knew were the kids from church, and he was nothing like them. The main difference was that he was funny and didn't care about being good all the time. He didn't really care about anything, which was a nice change after being surrounded by people my whole life who'd start praying for you if they heard you wiped your butt backward. It was fun to not feel like a boring homeschooled kid for once. He made me feel like I could be someone besides the person I'd always been, someone besides the person everyone else thought I was.

OLIVIA

I remember that first burst of energy when the pills kicked in. I remember all of a sudden not feeling like the awkward, shy, chubby girl I had always been. I felt like I could do anything. It became easier to do all the things I was supposed to do—it was easier to lose weight because I was never hungry; it was easier to stay at the top of my class because I suddenly felt smarter and sharper and I could stay up later to do homework. Those little magic pills made it easier to be perfect.

JASON

Everyone says alcohol is an acquired taste, but I can tell you that I loved it the moment I tasted that first beer. I loved everything about it.

EVA

The truth is, the girl wanted to feel something else, to be somewhere else, to get out of her body. The truth is, that was the best part. Do you know what it feels like to become someone new? Do you know what it feels like to do something as easy as swallow a tiny little pill and then be transformed into someone you don't hate?

CHRISTOPHER

I don't know how these

art projects are supposed to help us, but they're fun, so I'm not complaining. But Olivia's sitting over there in the corner with smoke coming out of her ears because they won't let her use activity hour to do her homework. It's fine with me if she thinks she's better than us, but I wish they'd figure out a way to make her happy, because her frowning all the time is making me anxious. The way I see it, they should just let her go somewhere else to be her crazy self and leave us lowly peasants to crawl around sticking our fingers together with glue.

You want to know what she said in Group this morning? I thought she was going to get murdered, the way everyone was looking at her, even Shirley. Imagine her sitting there all straight, with her hands folded in her lap, looking down on everyone and saying this: "How is it better for my recovery to sit on the floor doing art projects instead of using the activity hour to do my homework? I understand that most patients probably need to have all of their time structured, but I'm not like them. It's not like I'm a stoner loser who's flunking out of my mediocre public school. I don't need the kind of coddling they do." I swear to God, she really said that.

But wait, it gets worse. Then she was like, "Why does this place insist that I'm like everyone else here? Is it so you don't have to work so hard? I suppose it does make your job easier if you don't have to think of us as individuals. You can just give us the same cookie-cutter treatment regardless of whether or not it actually helps. I understand that you've probably never had a patient actually ask you for permission to do their homework. But it's not like I'm asking to skip activity hour to take a nap or smoke a cigarette." I'm not even exaggerating.

Then Eva was like, "How does it feel to be such a fucking snob?" like it's her job to put everyone in their place, and Olivia was like, "I'm not a snob. But let's be honest—I *am* different. I'm just stating the facts." And Eva just sat there kind of smug like she'd known Olivia was going to say that, and everybody just looked at each other like they couldn't believe what was happening, and Shirley just kind of smiled and said, "Time's up. See you all tomorrow."

So there she is, sitting here with everyone else, working on her "soul box" like she's not even worried about everyone wanting to kill her. They have this woman, Ingrid, come in and do "art therapy" with us twice a week, which in my opinion is the best thing we do in here, and I wonder what kind of college gives degrees for that and what kind of classes you have to take to get certified to teach drug addicts how to use glitter and construction paper, because that would be a pretty awesome job, if you ask me.

Dr. Ingrid—I don't know if she's actually a doctor, but I like the sound of it—she gave us one Plexiglas box each to decorate so it looks like our soul. Then we're supposed to stick our bad memories and thoughts in it—pictures, letters, old drug paraphernalia, scraps of paper with a fear or personality defect written on it. Then the magic box takes these bad things away so we don't have to store them inside anymore. That's the idea, anyway. I hope it works.

In case you're wondering, my soul box is going to be purple with white polka dots and blue glitter. I have a lot to put into it, including depression, which I've just been informed that I have. I saw the doctor today and he put me on antidepressants because my roommate found me crying in bed last night and it freaked him out. I told the doctor I just feel sad for no reason, which is pretty much the truth, and he said I'm depressed, which is common in people withdrawing from amphetamines, which is what crystal meth is, in case you didn't know. He said I should talk to Olivia, because she's probably going through the same thing from her diet pills, and I was like, "Yeah, like that's going to happen."

I wonder if it bothers Olivia that she's sitting alone. I guess we're not in here to make friends, but it's sure a lot more fun if you do. I swear she's been cutting that piece of black construction paper for, like, half an hour. I'll admit, it is pretty hard to cut a straight line since they only give us dull baby scissors so we can't use them as weapons or suicide devices. But it's like she's obsessed, like she's punishing that piece of paper for not being straight enough.

Kelly's across the room with Jason, and Lilana's already had to tell them twice to not sit so close. Me and Eva are in the opposite corner with the annoying Hippie Girl from a different Group who's always following Eva around. Eva's taking this assignment very seriously. After Ingrid explained the project and sent us on our way, Eva was the first to jump at the supply box and grab all the good stuff. I had no idea she could move so fast. Funny how excited she got about this art project, since she doesn't ever seem to care about anything. She's surprising like that, like one minute she's all quiet and mean and self-righteous, and the next minute she's all curled up in the corner writing in her journal and looking like she's going to cry. I guess she's one of those artsy kind of people with a bunch of layers like an onion, which probably explains why I can't figure her out. Maybe the secrets are in that journal she carries with her everywhere. Seriously, I never see her anywhere without it. It's nice that she has something to care about like that. I wonder what mine would be. I guess it's supposed to be Jesus, but I'd be lying if I said it was. Don't tell my mom.

Olivia took the corner behind the Ping-Pong table because she probably figured it would be the most private place in the room. Too bad that's also where the Scary Guys always sit. She's sitting there trying to pretend like she doesn't notice them sitting a few feet away from her, which, believe me, I know is impossible. Everyone notices them, whether they want to or not. People don't talk about it, but it's obvious we're all a little scared of them. Sure, we all have problems, but these guys are a million times worse. There's Gas Man, the huffer from Alaska who has killed so many brain cells he has slurred speech and permanent hearing loss; there's the Compulsive Liar, who's always trying to start fights with everyone; there's the Satan Worshipper, who will most likely end up a serial killer; and then there's their leader, the unspoken king of this place, the Heroin Addict.

Everyone says he had to stay in a hospital to detox for a week before coming here. The rumor is he lived on the streets before that, where he actually committed violent crimes to support his habit. I overheard two girls say he escaped from a mental hospital. Someone else said he was in jail. He's never allowed on any outings, even though no one's actually seen him break any rules. It's just all so mysterious—he must have parents somewhere, right? And they must have money, or else he wouldn't be here. I mean, let's face it. This place is kind of a country club as far as rehabs go.

Just being near him makes me nervous. Poor Olivia. If she got up now, it'd be obvious she was trying to get away from them and she'd be just asking to be humiliated. So she's trying to be invisible and working on her soul box, gluing that piece of paper so it's perfectly straight, and pressing out all the bubbles. Meanwhile, the Scary Guys are just a few feet away from her, and Gas Man is sculpting a penis out of pipe cleaners.

"This girl was probably twelve," the Heroin Addict says. "Even though she said she was sixteen." He's leaning back like he's totally relaxed, like he's on the beach instead of in rehab. "Some dude brought her over to where I was squatting, said he found her in an alley crying about how she just ran away from home because her brother was fucking her."

Yes, he really said that. At first I was totally horrified by the way people talk in here, but now I'm kind of used to it. It's like they're always trying to shock you or prove how tough they are, but the truth is that most everyone is from the suburbs and the only real danger they've ever been in has to do with the chemicals they put into their bodies. Anyway, then the Heroin Addict says: "Heard that shit before. That's what all the new little runaways say. Their brother, their dad, their fucking priest, whatever. All I know is they cry too damn much. And this girl was lying. No one had fucked her before. You know what I mean. She bled all over the fucking place."

You see what I mean by scary? The Heroin Addict makes everyone else look like amateurs. And Olivia just keeps on sitting there, cutting her piece of paper and pretending like she isn't listening. The Heroin Addict keeps on talking: "She's all young and stupid and never done anything in her life, and there's these beakers over by the window," and then Gas Man goes, "What's a beaker?" and Heroin Addict says, "Those glass things scientists put shit in." Compulsive Liar asks, "Where'd you get them?" and Heroin Addict says, "Dude, I don't know. That's not the fucking point," and then Satan Worshipper looks up from the demons he's drawing and makes a sound like a horse laughing.

Heroin Addict continues: "So there's these beakers full of cum, cuz me and my buddy jacked off into them the day before."

Yes, you heard right. He actually said that. Me and Eva and the annoying Hippie Girl look at each other like we threw up in our mouths a little. But guess what? It gets worse. Then he says, "And this girl's dying to get fucked up. She kept begging me to let her shoot up, but I was like, no fucking way I'm sharing with you when you're just gonna puke all over the place and probably piss yourself. So I told her the beakers were full of this really good stuff my friend made that was even better than heroin. And she was all horny to try it. So I tied off her arm and shot the bitch up with my cum."

Olivia's face is totally white, and she looks like she's about to lose her mind. Then Dr. Ingrid says it's break time, and the Scary Guys get up, and Heroin Addict kicks Olivia's shoe, and she looks up, and they're all standing there smiling. Heroin Addict says, "Like my story, little girl?" and they all laugh and walk outside to the fenced-in smokers' patio, and activity hour is over. Ingrid's cleaning up and Lilana's yelling at someone on the patio, and Olivia's just sitting there shaking. She's alone and scared and trapped in this place with a bunch of crazy people and no friends, and I know the Christian thing would be to go over and talk to her, but she gets up and walks up the stairs even though they're off-limits, and I don't try to stop her. I just get up and follow the smokers outside and try not to feel bad for not being nice to her. You may think that's mean, and you're probably right, but really, would you want to go talk to someone who thinks you're beneath them?

GROUP

SHIRLEY: Olivia, I hear you're isolating.

OLIVIA: What?

SHIRLEY: And you're not eating.

OLIVIA: Who told you that?

SHIRLEY: Oh, I have spies.

OLIVIA: I'm not isolating. I just need time to do my homework. You guys don't give enough time, so I have to take every chance I get.

SHIRLEY: Is that also your excuse for rearranging all of Kelly's stuff last night?

OLIVIA: No, I—What? Kelly, you told her that?

KELLY: No. I mean, yes. I mean, I told some people about how you moved my shit around. You have to admit it's kind of weird.

SHIRLEY: Olivia, how does it make you feel that Kelly called your behavior weird?

OLIVIA: I don't care. Can we change the subject?

SHIRLEY: Do you think your behavior's weird?

OLIVIA: I just want to do my homework. What's wrong with that?

SHIRLEY: And Kelly's shoes?

OLIVIA: I'm sorry.

KELLY: Apology accepted. We don't really have to talk about this.

SHIRLEY: Olivia, it's common for amphetamine users to exhibit obsessive-compulsive behavior. But the fact that you're continuing to exhibit this behavior several days after you last took pills makes me think there's something much deeper that we need to deal with.

OLIVIA: I won't touch Kelly's shoes again.

SHIRLEY: This is not about Kelly's shoes. It's the not eating, the homework, the isolating. You're trying to control everything around you. And that's just asking for disaster.

OLIVIA: I don't understand what's so wrong about wanting to do my goddamned homework. What's wrong with you people? Just because I'm focused and give a shit about my life and want to succeed, you think there's something wrong with *me*? Just because I'm different from all the losers in here?

CHRISTOPHER: Losers?

JASON: Whoa. Perfect girl said "shit."

EVA: Calling us losers is not the way to get us on your side.

OLIVIA: I'm sorry. I didn't mean that. Christopher, I don't think you're a loser.

CHRISTOPHER: I am kind of a loser.

SHIRLEY: Olivia, listen to me. I know you're in pain. Everyone in here is in pain. You don't have some sort of exclusive right to it just because you think you have the most to lose.

OLIVIA: I didn't say that. I didn't mean that at all.

JASON: Dude, Olivia, you're being kind of a bitch.

SHIRLEY: Dude, Jason, shut it.

JASON: Yes, sir.

SHIRLEY: Olivia, nothing's ever going to change for you until you let go of some of your control. Do you understand?

OLIVIA: No.

SHIRLEY: You don't live in the same world everyone else does. And it's not because you're rich or because of who your daddy is. It's because you've constructed this imaginary universe where you're the boss of everything. And it's killing you. Do you see that? Do you see how dangerous it's become?

OLIVIA: I know I have a problem with the diet pills. That's what I'm in here to fix, right? Isn't that what you guys are always trying to tell us? That it's the addiction that made us the way we are?

SHIRLEY: Getting rid of the drugs doesn't get rid of all the other ways you learned to deal with the world. It's not that easy.

KELLY: Oh my God, she's crying.

CHRISTOPHER: It's okay, Olivia.

SHIRLEY: Here's the deal, Olivia. From now on you will not be allowed in your bedroom alone. You will be required to spend each entire mealtime in the cafeteria. I have instructed the ACs to make sure you eat. You are not allowed to sit alone during activities. You must raise your hand to speak at every recovery meeting you attend. You are only allowed to work on homework during the allotted one hour we give you each day—

OLIVIA: But—

SHIRLEY: No buts. I'm in charge here, not you. You need to get used to that. The ACs have been instructed to keep your books and papers locked in the nurse's office.

OLIVIA: Shirley, you can't—

SHIRLEY: I can do anything I want. I am the counselor. You are the patient. There are more important things than grades, my dear. Your life, for instance. And once that's covered, your sanity is pretty damn important. Now, the rest of you, you have responsibilities here too. You may not like Olivia. You may think she's conceited and stuck-up, and you're probably right. But the deal is, if she doesn't get help now, she will die. This is not a joke. This isn't summer camp where you're just playing at recovery. This is a therapeutic community, and you have a responsibility to your community member whether you like it or not. Kelly, you are Olivia's roommate, and I am designating you her permanent buddy while you're both here. You must know where she is at all times. If she shows any unhealthy behavior, you must tell an AC immediately.

KELLY: Are you serious?

SHIRLEY: Do you want her to die?

KELLY: Jesus, Shirley. Of course not.

SHIRLEY: The rest of you, it is your responsibility to keep an eye on her during all group functions. If she's isolating, be with her. If you can't find her or she's not eating, tell an AC. If she's trying to organize things obsessively, call her on it. If she doesn't stop, tell an AC.

JASON: So you're basically telling us to tattle on her?

SHIRLEY: I'm telling you to give a shit about someone besides yourself for once in your life, and do what you have to do to help her. Is that okay with you, Jason?

JASON: Yeah. I mean, of course. Yes.

SHIRLEY: Everyone?

KELLY: Yes.

EVA: Yes.

CHRISTOPHER: Absolutely.

SHIRLEY: Olivia. How does it feel to have everyone commit to helping you?

OLIVIA: I don't know.

KELLY: Shirley, stop making her cry.

SHIRLEY: Olivia, how do you feel?

OLIVIA: Scared.

SHIRLEY: Good. That's a start. That's a very good start.

PERSONAL ESSAY

CHRISTOPHER

I guess one interesting thing about me is that my mom is fat. I mean *really* fat. Like morbidly obese. She can barely walk from our front door to the car in the driveway. Our church installed benches on the path from the parking lot just so she could sit down at regular intervals so she won't get too exhausted on her way to the door. She sleeps in what's supposed to be the living room on a king-size bed because she can't get up the stairs to the second floor, where the bedrooms are. Which is good for me, I guess. I've had the whole second floor to myself for as long as I can remember. I think the last time she came up there was when I was nine. I guess obesity does have its benefits.

OLIVIA

My older brother, Adam, started learning Latin at age four. Same with Jeffrey and the violin. Janice always reminds me how stubborn I was at that age, how brilliance wasn't as easy with me. She says I'd throw tantrums whenever it was time to go to what she refers to as my "augmentations" (which I believe normal people call "after-school activities"). I don't remember the moment I made the decision to accept the ballet and piano lessons, the speech and math tutoring. I don't remember the supposedly rebellious time before that, when I fought to stay unexceptional. All I remember is knowing, from the moment I could understand anything, that I had to be special like everyone else in my family. But along with that understanding came the realization that there wasn't really anything special about me. I think I was five. Maybe six. I just know I've been faking it for a really long time.

EVA

This world is not built for perfection. That is the first lesson. So God invented things like cancer to put us in our place. No one is innocent. God takes beautiful women away from their daughters, takes a father's soul with her, and leaves a ghost to raise a girl and teach her how to be empty. And then God makes you choose. This is the second lesson. He puts broken things in your path and calls it free will. And then you are told to pick the lesser of two evils, so you drink the poison that promises the slower death because anything is better than staying empty. Do you remember? Do you remember the world before the poison?

KELLY

We went to Disneyland once when I was twelve. My family doesn't have a bunch of money to throw around like everyone else in here, so it was a pretty big deal for us to go to Disneyland. The trip was really for my twin sisters, Shayla and Nicole, because they were seven and I was twelve and way too old for it to be any fun. I remember being really angry about it, about how our first real vacation in I don't know how long had to be for them. It couldn't be something I wanted to do. Nothing could ever be about me. So of course I decided I had to make the trip miserable for everyone, because that's the kind of shitty thing I do.

JASON

When I was six, I fell off my bike and broke my arm. Dad laughed at me. Told me to be a man and take the pain. When I was seven, we moved to Seattle from Kentucky. The kids in my class made fun of my southern accent. So I beat them up. I got sent home and my mom apologized to the principal. But my dad was proud. He looked me in the eye and smiled, like I'd finally done something right for once.

When I was eight, my mom got rushed to the hospital in the middle of her birthday party because of "dehydration." They gave her an IV and everything. But I knew it was because she drank too much. Nobody talked about it. Funny how her "fainting" looks the same as when I pass out. Funny how the nice nurses gave her fluids and a room with a view, but the drunks in the gutter have to wake up with puke all over themselves.

KELLY

We're lying on the floor

of a dark room listening to elevator music. Boys and girls lie in rows less than two feet away from each other, and we're told we're not supposed to touch anyone. This is worse than movie nights. You can practically feel the sexual tension in the air. The AC in charge looks and sounds like an ex–porn star, and she's saying things like "Close your eyes" and "Relax" and "Imagine yourself in a beautiful place," and I don't even want to know what kind of beautiful place the guys are imagining. I would like someone to explain to me how this is supposed to help me stay sober.

They call this "meditation hour," but my guess is it's what they throw into the schedule when they can't find anything better for us to do. We're all crammed together on the floor like sardines, and I'm just waiting for this to turn into some kind of orgy. Jason's only a couple of feet away. I could reach my arm out and touch him right now if I wanted to. I wonder if he's thinking of me, if he realizes how easy it'd be to touch me. How is anyone supposed to relax under these conditions?

The Sexy AC is practically purring: "Feel the warm air on your skin. Imagine you're lying on a bed of feathers. Take in a deep breath. Now breathe out." I wonder how many guys in here have boners.

The only one who's not lying down is that annoying Hippie Girl. She asked if she could sit in the "lotus position," and the Sexy AC practically gave her a standing ovation. "Of course, if you've found that that's your most open physical state for meditation." Then Hippie Girl went over to the wall and sat with her legs crossed weird and her hands turned up on her knees, with this smug look on her face like she's way more enlightened than everyone else in here. She'd actually be really pretty if she shaved her armpits and put on some makeup and wore clothes that fit. She'd probably be the hottest girl in here. I wonder if she knows that but chooses to look the way she does instead. I wonder what makes some girls work so hard at being pretty, while others don't seem to care at all.

Classical music is playing on the portable stereo. It's that song they always play at weddings. I think it's called "Taco Bell Cannon" or something like that. Olivia's on the other side of the room, but I swear I feel her stress all the way over here. What do they call it? Vibes? Her vibes are stressing me out. What she needs is to smoke a joint and get real mellow. I can't believe she was addicted to speed. I do not want to see what that looked like. Hopefully it had the opposite effect on her, like how Ritalin and Adderall calm down people with ADD.

Eva's a couple people away from me, lying perfectly still, and I wonder what she's thinking about. She hardly ever says anything, and when she does it's usually bitchy, but I don't think she's really as mean as she wants everyone to think she is. More than anything else, I think she's sad, but maybe she thinks mean looks better than sad. Maybe she thinks it makes her look stronger.

"Go to your place of relaxation," Sexy AC says. "Breathe the fresh air. Do you smell fresh-cut grass? Flowers? The sea?" All I smell is this nasty carpet and somebody's BO.

"Look around you. What do you see?" I don't know. My eyes are closed. I don't see anything. My bedroom? The kitchen? The basement? No, those are definitely not my places of relaxation. Nowhere in my house is. Neither is school or my car or probably anywhere I'd have to spend time with myself. There's just nowhere *that* far away.

I remember going to summer camp once, when I was nine. It was the only time I've ever been anywhere on my own, without my parents or my sisters. It was the only trip that was ever just mine, where I didn't have to share the spotlight with Shayla and Nicole. Pretty much all the other kids in my cabin were homesick and cried the first couple of nights and had to call their parents. It was this big production with the counselors taking them to the phones at the office, trying to keep them calm when they were all freaking out. I couldn't understand what they were so upset about. I was thrilled to be on my own and away from home. So I left. While they were all pissing their pants waiting for their turn at the phone to call their parents, I just walked away. I went down to the beach and found a nice spot under a tree, and sat down and looked out at the water, and everything was finally quiet. But not just quiet like no cars and no city noise kind of quiet, but quiet like all the noise inside shut up for a minute too, all those voices you carry with you that have an opinion about everything you do. I remember the inside of my head feeling clean, and I could actually stand my own company for once. In those few moments I felt like maybe I wasn't so bad after all. The sun was setting and painting everything yellow-orange, and the boats were rocking like something breathing, and the air felt just right, and for once in my life my skin fit perfectly.

I remember thinking I wanted to stay there forever. I wished all those girls in my cabin would take forever talking to their parents. Because in that place, in that moment, I had nothing to worry about. I didn't have to make anyone happy. I didn't have to worry about making anyone mad. I could just listen to the bugs and watch the lake slowly change to a different shade of orange, and it felt like I could breathe for the first time.

The AC says, "Breathe." I smell pine needles and salt water. She says, "Tense your muscles for five seconds—five, four, three, two, one. Now relax." And all of a sudden I feel my skin melting off, dead weight sinking into the floor, and I imagine myself lying on a boat in that water, drifting slowly out with the tide, and no one wants anything from me, and I have everything I'll ever need.

CHRISTOPHER

We just started talking,

and my mom's already crying. You see what I have to deal with?

"Oh, honey, it's so good to finally talk to you," she says over the phone. "I just don't understand why they wouldn't let you call before."

"They're doctors, Mom," I tell her. "They know what they're doing." I know this is what she needs to hear, but I'm not quite sure I believe it either. Last night after dinner we watched a couple episodes of a reality show involving a one-legged drug addict prostitute. First of all, that's just crazy. Second of all, I don't see how it's supposed to help us get sober. Third of all, is that really the best they can do with all the money they're getting paid to fix us?

"Are you praying?" Mom says. "Are you reading your Bible?"

"Yes, Mother." I should tell her I'm leading Bible study workshops with the Heroin Addict and the Satan Worshipper. I wonder what she'd think of that.

"That's my good boy," she says. "That's my good, sweet boy."

There's only one phone for patients, and we're only allowed to use it at a specific time on two designated days per week. It's stuck out here in the middle of the hall by the nurse's office, in a little cubicle with no doors, and walls that only go halfway to the ceiling, and I'm holding the receiver as close to my ear as possible to make sure no one can hear my mom blubbering on the other end of the line, because you can never be too careful in here. Can you imagine what kind of torture the Scary Guys would come up with if they heard this conversation? They'd probably strip me naked and put me in diapers and shove a pacifier into my mouth for being such a baby.

"We're praying for you, Christopher," she says. "We all are. Pastor Tom. All your friends at church."

"But they all think I have mono," I remind her.

"They're praying for you to be healed, sweetie," she says. "It's all the same in God's eyes."

Really, Mom? Staying at an imaginary relative's house because I'm sick with mono is the same as being in rehab for crystal meth addiction?

"Are they treating you all right?" she asks. "Are they feeding you enough?"

"Yes, Mom. Everything's fine."

"They're not hurting you, are they? The other kids in there?"

"No, of course not. Everyone's pretty nice."

"I'm just worried, Christopher. I don't like the idea of you being in there with a bunch of . . ."

"Drug addicts?"

"Oh," she says, like this is the first she's heard of it. "I think we made a mistake sending you there. We should have waited for a spot to open up at one of the Christian places. I should talk to Pastor Tom again. Maybe he can pull some strings." Her voice is getting higher and faster, like she's going to blow her top any second. I can just see her wringing her hands and sweat beading on her face as she contemplates the kinds of unsavory people I must be spending time with here. "You don't belong there, do you, honey? With those people? Do you even know if they're Christians?"

"I don't know, Mom. It hasn't really come up." I look around to make sure no one's listening. Eva's too busy arguing with the nurse about something, and Jason and Kelly are down the hall whispering pornographic things to each other, but I swear Mom's voice is coming through the loudspeakers and everyone can hear her and I'm going to be more of a laughingstock than I already am.

"You're not like those people, Christopher." I can hear the tears coming back. "You're a good boy. You belong at home with me. You should be going to church. Isn't that right? Honey?"

"I don't know."

"Of course you do, Christopher. You know you're nothing like those kids in there."

I don't say anything for a while. It's strange not looking at her when we're having a conversation. Right now I should be seeing her sad eyes begging me to say the right thing and to assure her that everything's fine and there's nothing to worry about and I'm her perfect little angel always. But all I see is the wall of this cubicle and the painted-over graffiti of penises and pot leaves and drug dealers' phone numbers. I can hear her breathing. I've never noticed how loud and kind of disgusting it sounds, like her lungs are wet, like she has to cough something up.

"Maybe I am," I say.

"Maybe you are what?" she says.

"Maybe I am like the kids in here." I don't know where this comes from, but I know it has something to do with me being here, and her being there, and the miles of distance between us.

"Don't be silly, Christopher," she says.

"I'm a drug addict, Mom." Wow. It feels good to say it. *I'm a drug addict, I'm a drug addict, I'm a drug addict, I'm a drug addict.*

"Christopher, don't."

"I'm a drug addict. I'm addicted to crystal meth."

"Oh, Jesus, please help my boy."

I'm being cruel. I shouldn't be scaring her like this. I should be telling her I'll bake her two dozen cookies and we'll sit on her bed together while I read her Psalms and massage her shoulders. I should be assuring her that everything's going to be okay and I'm going to come home soon and everything's going to be just like it was when I was five years old. But I would be lying. Nothing's going to be the same. Once the truth is out, no amount of denial is going to put it back.

"Mom," I say. "I'm in rehab." I talk slowly to make sure she hears it.

"Pastor Tom says everyone in youth group misses you. They pray for you at the beginning of every meeting. You know, they're doing a canned food drive for the homeless this year. Your friend Lynn is helping me clean out the pantry. Do you think we want to keep a can of water chestnuts? I can't for the life of me think what I would have wanted water chestnuts for. Pastor Tom's making sure someone comes over in the afternoon every day to help me. Isn't that nice of him? But of course no one is as good a help as you, honey."

I wonder what my mom would say if she saw all the stuff that's been carved in this wall, all the sketches of body parts and references to sex acts, the various profanities. I don't even know what some of these things mean.

"Don't you think that's nice?" she says.

Is it weird that this graffiti is kind of turning me on?

"Christopher? Hello?"

"Mom," I say, "I'm not as perfect as you think I am."

"What are you talking about?" She's trying to laugh, but it doesn't sound right. "Christopher, honey, don't be silly. You'll always be perfect to me."

"Even if I'm a drug addict?"

"Christopher." She is not laughing anymore.

I don't know why I'm talking to her like this, but I can't stop. It's suddenly so easy. Is this how normal teenagers talk to their parents? Is it our job to try to hurt them?

"I have to go, Mom," I say. It's time for dinner. Everyone's heading into the cafeteria.

"No, honey. Just stay on a little while longer."

"Tell everyone I say hi."

"Christopher, wait."

"I love you, Mom."

I hang up and feel a surge of electricity. I suddenly feel the air around me, the empty space that proves I'm not attached to my mother. A cord's been cut and I'm here, alone. It is me deciding to stand up now. It is me deciding to walk.

Maybe I'm not who my mother thinks I am. Maybe I'm not who anyone thinks I am. Eva's waving at me from the end of the hall. She thinks I'm somebody worth talking to. Maybe I am.

DRUG & ALCOHOL HISTORY QUESTIONNAIRE

QUESTION #2:

Tell the story of what happened that caused you to come to treatment, the drugs and the amounts, and the thoughts and feelings you had at the time.

KELLY

It was Friday. Saturday morning, actually. I had been drinking and doing coke all night, which was pretty normal. I guess I had a gram of coke that night—really good stuff—and God, I don't even know how many drinks. At some point we started drinking straight from the bottle, so I lost track.

CHRISTOPHER

I don't know how long I could have kept going. It's not like I was ever going to get caught. My mom probably couldn't make it up to the second floor if she wanted to, plus there's no way she would ever intentionally destroy her delusion that everything is perfect and fine. Todd sure wasn't going to tell anyone he was smoking meth with the weird homeschooled kid down the street.

OLIVIA

I was running. Janice said I couldn't just be skinny, I had to be toned. She says skinny girls with cellulite are worse than fat ones.

JASON

I'm sure my parents already told you about that at my intake. Nobody wants my side of the story. Next question.

EVA

Her father could have chosen any moment to start paying attention, any one of millions of moments in those almost three years. No one knows why he chose the one he did, that one particular moment when nothing out of the ordinary happened, when he and the girl had just been going about their regular lives, living in the same house, not getting in each other's way, he forgetting in his way, she forgetting in hers.

CHRISTOPHER

My mom would have probably stayed in denial until I shriveled up and died. I'd still be her little angel even if I was seventy pounds and splayed out on the floor of my bedroom, twitching and scratching myself to death because of the imaginary bugs under my skin.

OLIVIA

I was running, and I started feeling dizzy, which was pretty normal. I just kept running. I was going to run right through the feeling, because I knew that if I stopped I wouldn't be able to start again. That's what you have to do when things get hard—just keep going, even if you think it's going to kill you.

KELLY

I guess I blacked out. I don't remember much about that night. I don't remember much about most Friday nights.

EVA

The father became a hermit and the girl lived in fog.

Sometimes others would join her, and the hermit would stay in his cave, leaving them untended. But mostly she was alone, and mostly she was grasping at smoke and the magic pills that kept her forgetting, that allowed her to pretend she was in some far-off land. And still the hermit stayed in his cave, pretending the same thing.

JASON

I know you already heard about Jessica. You probably have all the police reports in my file. That's all you need to know.

EVA

This scene does not end with fireworks. The girl did not get arrested, or overdose, or any number of things that happen to girls like her. She just finally got caught. But the truth is, she never really tried that hard to hide it. The truth is, the father just decided one day to open his eyes. And there she was, right in front of him. There she was, right where she'd been the whole time.

KELLY

It was just a regular Friday night. That's the weird thing. I drove home drunk and high all the time. But this time, I don't know, maybe I'd had a little too much. Maybe I hadn't eaten enough. Maybe it was just really bad luck.

JASON

I was drunk. Big surprise. I came home after school because my mom was making me watch Jessica. She had one of her stupid military wife parties where they sit around drinking pink wine and talking about dumb housewife shit. So I got home and she left, and it was just me and my three-year-old sister and nothing to do. So I made myself a drink. I have this giant plastic Huskies cup that fits, like, three or four drinks in it. I had a couple of those.

CHRISTOPHER

I could have probably kept going and going until I died. No one was going to stop me. No one was going to do anything.

OLIVIA

I got dizzier and dizzier. And my chest started to hurt and everything got blurry and I couldn't breathe. It felt like there was a belt around my chest that kept getting tighter and tighter, and I just couldn't keep going, and I tried to keep going, but then I knew I had stopped, I had finally stopped, I was falling, and everything was going to be different from that moment forward.

KELLY

When I woke up, the cops were in my living room and my mom was crying and my dad was pacing back and forth, and the first thing I thought was, *My sisters. Oh my God, something happened to my sisters.*

EVA

He saw her one day out of the corner of his eye, and the girl had changed into something unrecognizable. She was no longer a small, sweet thing. He had not noticed all the clues she'd left for him to find, not her silence, not the shadows she hid behind. But that is to be expected when a mother dies and leaves a father to finish raising a half-woman, when he turns his home into a cave and refuses to come out. It is hard to see anything from inside a cave.

CHRISTOPHER

I hadn't slept in three days and I was scared. I had always managed to keep things under control, but it was getting harder and harder. It felt like there were all these things piling up, all these secrets, and I felt like I was going to explode.

JASON

I was drinking and looking around on the Internet, and Jessica was just playing on the floor with her toys. And I needed another drink, so I went downstairs to the den, where the bar is. There are a lot of stairs. And they're wood. Hard. And I forgot to close the baby fence thing. And it was open. And Jessica was following me. I didn't know.

OLIVIA

I remember the sound of sirens. Someone pulling on my arm asking if I was okay. A dog's wet nose sniffing my neck. A growing crowd and a chorus of muted voices. "Is that the Cunningham girl?"

CHRISTOPHER

I was out of my mind, but I can remember sitting down on my mom's bed and deciding that I'd had enough. I think I said something like, "Mom, I think I'd like to go to rehab, please," and she just kept blinking at me. I remember the blinking. I told her I had a drug problem and I needed help, but I don't think I waited for a response. I just left her there blinking and went upstairs and fell asleep for two days.

EVA

The girl came home, and there he was, sitting at the dining room table that hadn't been used in almost three years, with her stash sitting on a plate in front of him, everything arranged in neat little piles like a grotesque Passover plate.

KELLY

The cops said I drove my car onto the neighbors' front lawn. I crushed their front porch and destroyed their prized rosebushes. I remember the nausea I felt when I looked next door, like the ground had suddenly disappeared and taken my stomach with it. I remember holding my breath, asking myself, *How can I not remember doing that?* I remember thinking, *What if those rosebushes had been people? What if that porch had been some little kid's bedroom?*

JASON

I remember the sound of her falling. I remember the soft *thump, thump, thump,* in slow motion, like that sound was the only thing that existed, like everything else was frozen. I was frozen. There was just the sound of her little body falling, like a sack of potatoes, like a baseball mitt. And then silence. That was the worst part. The silence.

OLIVIA

The doctor said I'd had a heart attack. I'm seventeen and I had a heart attack.

KELLY

I pretty much hid in my room the whole time I was waiting to go to court. My parents didn't even have to punish me, because I did it myself. I stopped going out. I stopped talking to my friends. Suddenly none of it seemed like that much fun anymore. But I thought my friends were going to at least make it hard for me, at least call and beg for me to come out. But they didn't. Not once. Everyone at school found out what had happened and tried to make it a joke, but when I didn't laugh with them, they were just like, "Bummer," and then they went off to have fun without me. No "Are you okay?" No "Do you need anything?" Not even good-bye.

EVA

It was usually so easy to be cruel to him, but there he was, exposed, without the protection of his cave, his face painted with a new devastation. And there was something else there too, something like fear, and the girl realized she was terrified too. The father said, "I found this in your room." And all the girl could say was "Yes."

OLIVIA

Everyone sent flowers. All of my mom's rich charity friends. All of Dad's business partners' wives. The hospital room was like a giant gaudy bouquet. The IV in the back of my hand itched. Fluids. I was dehydrated. And calories, the nurse said. I was malnourished. Then she shook her head and said under her breath, just loud enough that I could hear, "How can a rich white girl be malnourished?"

CHRISTOPHER

When I woke up and went downstairs, Pastor Tom was in the living room holding my mom's hand. She was crying softly and wouldn't even look at me. Pastor Tom said he'd made an appointment. He didn't mention what for. He told me to get dressed and grab something quick to eat on the way. I made some toast, plus a couple pieces for my mom. I hugged her and kissed her on the cheek, and she just sat there crying, and I knew she would never look at me the same again.

JASON

Jessica's out of the coma now. She came home just before I left for this place. Permanent brain damage, they say. She can't talk anymore. She can barely walk. She just sits there and looks out into space, like she's searching for something.

KELLY

The judge let me off easy. One look at my sad sweet family and I had his sympathy. Instead of juvie and a criminal record, I was ordered to go to rehab. So here I am. I guess I'm lucky.

EVA

The funny thing was, the girl wasn't really mad. She mourned her medicine flushed down the toilet, but there was a larger feeling, a foreign feeling, like she was almost happy that he'd sifted through her secrets, happy that he'd finally seen things of hers.

CHRISTOPHER

I e-mailed Todd before I left. He didn't even ask if I was okay. All he wrote back was, "Did you tell?" and I knew he wasn't talking about the drugs.

OLIVIA

It's hard to lie when doctors can do toxicity tests while you're unconscious. And it's impossible to think up a story when someone else beats you to it. I woke up to everyone knowing what chemicals were in my body, but no one had any clue how they'd gotten there, so they jumped to the natural conclusions.

I woke up to my father crying, wondering how his straight-A daughter could have succumbed to peer pressure, how I could have used his money to buy drugs off the street. I did not correct him. I did not tell him where the drugs were from. I glanced at my mother hiding behind him, and she couldn't meet my eyes. "I'm sorry," I told my father. "I'm sorry."

JASON

My mom's slap hurt worse than my dad's punches, his kicks to my side that cracked my rib. Because when she said "It should have been you," I knew she was right.

KELLY

Something is seriously wrong with Olivia. It's been days, and I don't think I've seen her smile once. How is that even possible? Even the most depressed person in the world has to smile sometimes. She's over there on her side of the room cleaning like her life depends on it. All we have to do is pick stuff off the floor and make our beds, but she's doing that thing where she lines up all her shoes so they're pointing in the exact same direction. I guess I'm supposed to be watching her so she doesn't do anything crazy, but how am I supposed to know? Everything she does looks crazy to me.

"Hey, Olivia," I say. I guess it won't hurt to be nice to her. And if I'm stuck in this room for the next twenty minutes,

I might as well talk to somebody. It's better than sitting on my bed and staring at the wall, which is pretty much the only other thing there is to do.

"What?" she says. She's tucking the sheets so tight that there are no wrinkles anywhere. Her sleeves are rolled up and I can see her tiny muscles straining against her skin and bones. God, she's skinny. She's pulling as hard as she can, and it looks like her arms could break.

"It's only a sheet," I tell her, but she says nothing.

She starts on the other corner. "Do you have a boyfriend?" I say.

"No." She doesn't even look at me. Aren't girls from families like hers supposed to have better manners than this?

"Have you ever had a boyfriend?"

"I don't think that's any of your business." She's adjusting the pillow so it's in the exact middle of the bed. She moves it an inch to the left, then about a half centimeter to the right.

"I bet you think I'm a slut, don't you?" I say. Now she looks at me. It takes her a while to say something.

"No, I don't think that. I don't really think anything."

"Liar," I say, but in a nice way. "I know what people think about me." I could be hallucinating, but I swear she relaxes a little. She almost looks me in the eye. "What's your dream guy like?" I ask her.

"I don't have a dream guy," she says.

"Are you a lesbian? It's totally cool if you are. My aunt Lorrie is a lesbian."

Back to angry face again. She's at the dresser now, taking out all her clean clothes. "No, I am not a lesbian."

"I didn't really think so," I say. She unfolds one of her sweaters, then refolds it and puts it back into the drawer.

"You know what's weird?" I say. "I don't really like hot guys." I think she just rolled her eyes, but I don't care. "I go out with all these hot guys, but they're assholes, you know?" I don't know why I'm telling her this. Maybe because I know she won't tell anyone. In order to gossip she'd actually have to talk to people.

"There's this guy in my history class I kind of like," I tell her. "I think he's in the drama club or something. He's kind of short and he's not really that cute, but he always seems happy. Like, genuinely happy, you know? Not happy like he's high or making fun of people; he just seems happy with himself and the way things are in the world. I did a group project with him one time and he was really nice, like he really listened when I was talking. I think he likes me, but I can't really tell. That's weird, you know? Usually I can totally tell when someone likes me."

Olivia shows no sign that she's heard anything I've said. Talking to her is only slightly better than talking to a wall.

She's on her knees now and moving something around under her bed. "Do you want help with that?" I ask her.

"No," she says to the floor. She's not wearing a belt, and her size double-zero jeans are riding low on her hips. I can see each vertebra of her spine sticking out of her back. She turns to get farther under the bed, and her jeans drop even lower, and I can see the bone of her hip. It's decorated with a dozen or so thin red lines, perfectly straight, perfectly parallel. If she were anyone else, I'd probably think it was some kind of weird pseudo-tribal tattoo. I guess I shouldn't be surprised that Olivia's a cutter, but it's scary to see it all of a sudden, her pain turned into these sad, precise scars. I feel like I should look away, like I have seen something way too intimate.

She turns around and catches me looking. Her face turns red and she pulls up her pants and crawls even farther under the bed.

"What are you doing under there?" I say. Just act like nothing happened.

"Nothing."

I don't know why, but I go over and sit on her bed.

"Don't mess up the sheets," she says.

"I'm not," I tell her.

"I'm just trying to keep everything organized," she says.

"You do that a lot, huh?"

"What?"

"Try to keep things organized."

She pulls herself out from under the bed and just sits there, looking straight ahead like she didn't even hear me.

"Why does everything with you always have to be so perfect?" I ask her.

"I don't know," she says, and all of a sudden she seems exhausted, like she can't keep her posture straight, like she barely has enough energy to keep her head up.

"It sounds hard," I say.

"What?"

"Being you."

She looks at me like I just offered her a million dollars but like she doesn't trust me, like she thinks I'm playing a trick on her and I'm going to take it back any second. I never thought I'd say this, but I guess I kind of feel sorry for Olivia. I wonder if anyone's ever really noticed how hard she's working and how crazy it's making her.

"You know what?" I say. "I think I can help you."

"How?"

"I am totally qualified to teach you how to be a slacker." She doesn't laugh. She doesn't even smile, which actually hurts my feelings a little. "Oh, lighten up," I say. "You're on vacation."

She sits up a little straighter, smooths out her sweater, and runs her fingers through her hair. There's definitely some pretty in there, something soft. But she blinks, and just like that, she's ice again.

"Are you going to tell?" she asks.

"About what? All your crazy organizing? Do you want me to tell?"

"What do you think?"

"What about the other thing?" I say. She acts like she didn't hear me. "I saw the cut marks, Olivia." She looks away, tugging on her sleeve. "Don't you think you need to talk about it?" She doesn't say anything. "Don't you think you need to talk about *something*?"

She pulls away and stands up, looks in the mirror and tucks the stray pieces of hair behind her ears. She runs her hand along the clothes in our shared closet, each hanger perfectly spaced.

"Hello?" I say, but she says nothing, just shuts the closet door and walks into the hall like I don't exist.

DRUG & ALCOHOL HISTORY QUESTIONNAIRE

QUESTION #3:

What were the negative consequences of your drinking and/or drug use? What problems have you had as a result?

self-destruction   hangovers

self-harm   humiliation

blackouts   overdoses

trouble in school   trouble with the law
trouble with my parents

loss of trust   loss of relationships

loss of respect

spent all my money on drugs   worthlessness

sadness

stole money for drugs

powerlessness

rage   had sex for drugs

shame

depression

unwanted sex   anxiety   suicidal thoughts

pregnancy   loss of control

STDs   liver damage

rape   abortion   heart damage

weight gain

lung damage

weight loss

guilt   brain damage

fear   anger   bad grades   shame

loss of ambition   shame

shame

PERSONAL ESSAY

CHRISTOPHER

Something I've realized since I've been here is that my world is very small. Like, freakishly small. Like, not normal. I've never been anywhere. My whole life I've pretty much stayed within a one-mile radius of my house in my crappy neighborhood of Renton. But it never really struck me as weird until now, because I guess everyone else I know is pretty sheltered too. I'm homeschooled, so the only other places I go are church every Sunday, Bible study every Wednesday night, and youth group every Tuesday and Saturday nights. All of these take place at my church, which is a five-minute walk from my house. Church, church, church. My entire life takes place between home and church. Church and home. Sometimes Mom will send me on an errand like to pick up milk at the corner store, which is three blocks away. But that's rare. Most everything we need gets delivered. My mom got a big personal injury settlement around the time my dad left when I was a baby, plus the government gives her money because she can't leave the house to go to work or anything, so that takes care of that. We're a very self-contained family.

OLIVIA

There's not much to say about me, really. My existence is defined by how I compare to everyone else in my family. Every year marks another handful of awards earned by my brothers, another promotion for my father, another article in the newspaper about my mother's fund-raising galas. And then there's me, invisible and "better-than-average." That would be good enough for most people, but not for me. "Average" is still in the title.

JASON

When I was nine, I broke a plate when I was washing the dishes and my dad whipped me with his belt until I bled. I didn't cry. I stood there, bent over the kitchen table with my naked ass in the air, getting whipped so bad it hurt to sit for a week. But I didn't cry. I don't have much to be proud of, but I'm proud of that.

EVA

This girl is a sixteen-year-old pothead and pill hound. It wasn't always like this. No. She was someone else once. There was sunshine and whispering grass. There were neighborhood parks with sandboxes too wholesome to be shat in by wandering cats. Clean sandboxes. That was the world. That was the first day. But on the second day, there was cancer. There was a mother, gone. On the third day, there was silence. There was a hole, bottomless. There was the girl, consuming everything in sight, trying to fill the hole. There was no one around to tell her to stop.

KELLY

You know those losers who dress up like cartoon characters and go around posing for pictures with kids? I pushed one over once. At Disneyland. Donald Duck, I think it was. He was posing for a picture with the twins, and I just walked up to him and pushed him as hard as I could. He fell onto his back, and his stumpy little arms and legs were flailing all over the place, and my sisters and all the other kids were crying, and parents were hugging them, comforting them like they'd just seen someone get murdered. And you could hear poor, stupid Donald screaming inside his giant costume head, and he couldn't get up even though other employees ran over and were trying to help him. So he ended up just taking off his Donald Duck head even though I'm sure it's probably totally forbidden, and there he was—this scruffy, fat, sweaty, panting man who looked more like a child molester than a cartoon duck. And I just stood there looking at my parents for a reaction, any reaction. But they were too busy comforting Shayla and Nicole, hugging and kissing them and telling them everything was going to be okay.

OLIVIA

Compared to everyone in here, I might as well be from a different planet. They don't know what it's like to be raised by a nanny, to only eat meals with my parents on holidays, to live in a house with a separate wing for the children. They don't know what it's like to have every minute of their day scheduled with some kind of mind-enriching activity. The only thing we have in common is the fact that we ended up here.

CHRISTOPHER

Every day of my life has been pretty much identical since the day I was born. I've always lived in the same house. I've always gone to the same church. The only difference is that the kids I know have gotten taller. I guess I'd call them my friends. I mean, I've seen them at church my entire life. But I'm not sure that's enough to make someone your friend. The way I see it, there's a world outside and there's a world inside, and those worlds are different. All these people I've known forever, they just live in the outside world. Todd's the only one who saw inside, just a little, but he probably didn't even notice.

EVA

Do you remember? Do you remember being solid? Do you remember life before the hole? Before you were empty and needed to be filled? There was a time when everything was enough. There was a time you didn't try to get out of your own skin. Remember.

KELLY

One of us could just

open the van door and jump out and start running. As soon as we stop at a stoplight, I could make my escape. I could hide in those trees over there. I could run into that housing development and they'd never find me. I could live off of garbage. I could sleep in a toolshed. I could bathe in the automatic sprinkler system that goes on every morning at six thirty on the dot, just in time to spray the paperboy, just in time to water the sidewalk that no one ever walks on.

Or I could just stay in my seat, secured in my seat belt, looking out the window, stuck between a church boy and an anorexic girl with OCD, in the middle seat of the middle row of a big old unmarked van, on the way to a meeting for recovering alcoholics.

I feel sorry for the old drunks in the church basement, the way we descend into their musty room like locusts, devouring their coffee and stale cookies when no one's looking, the way we whisper and giggle while they pour out their souls. This one's been sober twenty-one years. A lot of good it's done him. He may be sober, but he's still old and boring and smells like mothballs. He's talking about how he prays every morning as soon as he wakes up and makes a list of everything he's grateful for before he goes to bed. And in between? The same nothing every day. The same inconsequential existence, the same meaningless series of breaths bookended by empty ritual. Then sleep. Then the same thing the next day.

It does smell like mothballs in here. And decades of burnt coffee. The linoleum is cracked orange. Faded slogans line the walls with their dingy optimism. ONE DAY AT A TIME. EASY DOES IT. LET GO AND LET GOD. The plastic chairs squeak under familiar ancient asses.

The man is talking about how bad it got, about how he woke up every morning promising himself that day would be different. But he'd end up drunk just the same. And the shame built. The powerlessness. The ritual of insanity continued. You know you have a problem when you can't stop on your own. You know you have a problem when you lose everything but keep doing it anyway. That's when you require divine intervention. That's why we are here. There is God in these rooms. There is God in these old people and their years of sobriety and their slogans and their patronizing stares, their "Keep coming back," their "You kids are lucky to get this chance so young."

Yes, we're real lucky. I'm lucky to have slept with more guys than I can count; Jason's lucky for having a dad who beats him up every chance he gets; Christopher's lucky to have been raised in a horror movie; Olivia's lucky to be totally alone in the world; and Eva's lucky to have a dead mom and a clueless dad and an expensive habit that got her stuck in this basement on a Saturday night, surrounded by old men who have seen the light, hallelujah, now put a dollar in this basket, now raise your hand and say you're an alcoholic and talk about how God is doing for you what you could not do for yourself.

Okay, God. Here's one for you. Here's something I could not do for myself. I could not make my sisters healthy. I could not be good enough or pray hard enough or keep everyone smiling long enough to get the sickness out. I could not love them enough to make everything normal. How's that? What are you going to do now? Are you going to cure them? Are you going to make all my dreams come true? Are you going to make my parents love me as much as they love my sisters?

Or maybe you can do even better. Maybe you can make

time go backward, to before the drugs, before the sickness, before my sisters were even born, when I didn't have to share my parents' love with children who are so much more worthy. There's my mom, just like a movie, holding a warm tray of cookies just out of the oven. There I am, when I still had an appetite. There we are in a bright kitchen on a Sunday morning. The sound of birds chirping. The sun reflecting off of shiny clean pots and pans. The feeling that everything will be okay forever.

And here comes Dad in his bathrobe. He kisses us both on the cheek. Maybe we have a dog, a golden retriever who's sniffing at the table, drunk on the smell of cookies. We all laugh. We say "Oh, Goldie" in unison, and Dad says, "That silly dog."

And then what? After-school activities. Ballet. Soccer. Help with homework. Maybe I join the Girl Scouts. Maybe my hair is still brown instead of this blond dye job. Maybe I'm on the debate team or in drama club and I go to movies with my friends instead of snorting coke and having sex with guys so old it's illegal. Maybe I don't have to get drunk every day, because I tutor kids with learning disabilities and maybe I'm school treasurer and maybe my life is going somewhere and maybe everywhere I look I see rainbows.

And then what? Definitely not this. Definitely not

seventeen and in rehab, definitely not angry and scared and convinced that nothing will ever change. Not with that feeling in my stomach and my chest like I can't breathe, that feeling like a giant fist squeezing. And now they're telling me I have to get rid of the only thing that loosens its grip. That's the irony, isn't it? That's what these old men are trying to tell me with their sad stories and coffee breath. The thing that helped has become the thing that imprisons us. We keep feeding it and it keeps wanting more. This is a disease that tries to convince you that you don't have it. This is a disease where the medicine that gives relief is the same thing that kills you.

I have been sober for almost two weeks now. This morning after Group, I went into the bathroom and pinched myself with my fingernails until I drew blood, so I guess I'm just as crazy as Olivia now. I just had to do something to make the feelings stop. I had to do something to get away from myself. I would rather have done a line, a shot, pills, anything to leave this world for somewhere upside down. I have learned to make magic with chemicals, but I have lost all my tools. All I'm left with is this tight fist that keeps squeezing, that keeps me running toward anything I can do to loosen it, even if the relief is only temporary, even if the fist's grip just ends up tighter in the end.

Another old man raises his hand and introduces himself.

"My name's Larry, and I'm an alcoholic." You felt this once, didn't you, Larry? This strap across your chest, your hands behind your back, your ankles chained to the floor? Remember how it feels to have nowhere to go? When all you can do is just let the feelings consume you?

Tell me, when does this stop? When can I be like you, sitting in a church basement, content with these clichés and these rules and these steps and this sobriety? When is this liberation you keep talking about? Because I don't feel it. I'm two weeks sober and I'm locked up and I've lost control of everything. If this is recovery, I don't want it. If this is sobriety, I'd like my drugs back, thank you very much.

The meeting's over and we stand up and hold hands. We bow our heads and have a moment of silence for the alcoholic who still suffers. We say a prayer to a God I don't know. The old men shake hands, ask each other about their grandkids. And the kids mill around, waiting to be led out.

GROUP

SHIRLEY: How was the meeting last night?

JASON: It kind of sucked.

SHIRLEY: Well, luckily there are a lot of different meetings, so you can always try new ones until you find some that fit. I'm curious, though—why did the meeting suck?

JASON: It was a bunch of old guys.

SHIRLEY: They were too old? That was the problem?

JASON: No. I don't know. I just didn't relate. I don't have anything in common with a bunch of old drunks.

SHIRLEY: You're all addicts and alcoholics. That's something.

JASON: I guess. But my life's not anywhere near as bad as theirs were. Not even close.

SHIRLEY: Anyone else care to contribute?

KELLY: I kind of agree. It's not like I don't realize I have a problem with drugs and alcohol, but I haven't lost everything like they did. None of us are *that* bad.

SHIRLEY: Do you want to know what I think?

JASON: Do we have a choice?

SHIRLEY: Yes, you're right, none of you are that bad. Do you know why?

JASON: Because we're not addicts and alcoholics, and we can go home now?

SHIRLEY: Very funny. No. There are a couple reasons. Reason number one: your age. You haven't been using that long. The disease hasn't had as much time to destroy you, but that doesn't mean you don't have it. The fact that you're here proves that you've moved beyond drinking or using like a normal person. You've moved beyond recreational use. So, congratulations. You have earned a place in the club with those old drunks. Lucky for you, you don't have to wait for all the same terrible things that happened to them to happen to you. You get to stop now. Do you realize how lucky you are?

JASON: I guess so.

SHIRLEY: Olivia, did you ever have to go to a scary part of town to buy your drugs?

OLIVIA: What? No.

SHIRLEY: Did you ever have to rob someone to finance your addiction?

OLIVIA: Of course not.

SHIRLEY: Eva, you've never shot heroin, have you?

EVA: No.

SHIRLEY: Do you know why?

EVA: Because I'm not a junkie.

SHIRLEY: Oh, sure, and popping handfuls of pills or crushing up and snorting prescription opiates is totally fine.

JASON: Ha.

SHIRLEY: Listen to me. All of you. Listen very carefully.

Kelly, imagine you're a poor black kid. Now imagine you're drunk and high on cocaine and you run your mom's car into a house. What do you think happens to you?

KELLY: I don't know.

SHIRLEY: Do you think a judge will give you a slap on the wrist and tell your parents to send you to an expensive private rehab?

KELLY: No? I don't know.

SHIRLEY: And, Olivia, let's look at what happened to you. You get to tell people you fainted while you were jogging. But guess what? You OD'd. In the middle of the fucking street. Do you think if you lived in the ghetto and that happened, some nice neighbors would just help you home and your family could cover it up like nothing happened? And, Jason, can you still complain about being here when you consider the alternatives? What about juvie? Or what about becoming a ward of the state? Foster homes, group homes? What about being homeless?

JASON: Okay. We get it.

SHIRLEY: No, I don't think you do. If you think you don't have anything in common with those old alcoholics, then you must definitely think you have nothing in common with those people you so lovingly refer to as crackheads and junkies. But guess what? You have everything in common with them. They're just the poorer version of you. The only difference between cocaine and crack is the color of the user's skin and the amount of money in his wallet. None of you ended up here by accident. We don't take in every kid who's snuck wine at a bar mitzvah or inhaled once or twice. Listen to me: You do not drink or use like a normal person. You have moved beyond the point where you can *ever* drink or use like a normal person. If you don't believe me, fine, go ahead and try to prove me wrong. We're always open. I'm sure your parents would love to pay for another stay here. Hopefully you'll make it back. Hopefully you don't need to keep testing to see if you're like the ones who *don't* make it, the ones who OD and die on the streets, the ones who end up in jail, the ones who end up crazy and alone and living in a cardboard box. Or maybe you spend the rest of your life in and out of expensive rehabs, maybe you OD in a nice house or you pass out and drown in your pool. Maybe you die in a car accident while driving a really expensive car. What's the difference? Anyone have an idea? No? I'll tell you. The only things you have going for you are race and money and the fact that someone cares enough about you to get you help instead of just throwing you out on the street and letting you destroy yourself. If you're anything less than grateful, you're a fucking asshole and a waste of my time.

JASON: Wow.

CHRISTOPHER: I'm sorry, Shirley.

EVA: Christopher, you didn't even do anything.

CHRISTOPHER: But I feel bad.

EVA: Stop crying, Christopher.

CHRISTOPHER: I'm sorry.

EVA: Stop saying you're sorry.

OLIVIA: We're grateful, Shirley. I'm grateful.

JASON: I'm grateful too.

KELLY: We're all grateful.

SHIRLEY: Yeah, sure, we'll see about that.

KELLY

I'm supposed to feel
excited now, aren't I? I'm supposed to be giddy with girly
anticipation. But I'm not. I don't think I know what that feels
like. And I guess I've never even thought about that, never
realized something's missing.

I'm thinking about it now because I'm about to do
something really stupid. I'm waiting in the dark until the clock
strikes midnight, and then I'm going to put everything on the
line. I'm going to break the rules. And for what? I haven't been
able to figure that out in the almost two hours I've been lying
here in bed, listening to Olivia's breathing, listening to Lilana's
knitting in the hall.

Soon Lilana will check our room. She will make her way

down the girls' hall, and I will stuff my bed with clothes so it looks like I am sleeping. Then she will turn around and start her checks on the boys' hall. That's when I will make my run for the bathrooms. I will find the third shower room on the right. I will find him waiting for me, the boy I'm not even sure I like.

What is making me willing to do this? Sexual relationships between patients is forbidden. Getting caught means certain expulsion. What is making me willing to risk that, risk getting kicked out of this place even though I want to stay? This is the first time in I don't know how long that I've come even close to caring what happens next. I guess you could call that hope. Am I willing to give that up for a night with Jason? Does he mean that much to me?

No. Of course not. But that's not it. It's not about want or desire or how much he means to me. It's definitely not about love or anything resembling love. If I had to pick a word, I guess it would be habit, but that's not quite it either. This is just what I know how to do. It's what I've always done. I will sneak out tonight and meet Jason in the shower and risk getting kicked out of here because I don't know what else to do. This is who I am on the outside, so this must be who I am in here, too.

At school I have always hated the purity-ring girls. They

walk the halls so proudly because they've vowed not to have sex before marriage, like God loves them better than everyone else, like God loves them more because they made Him a promise that they would never be a girl like me. I hate them for that. I hate them for their voices, for their ability to say no. I hate them for believing their bodies are worth something, that sex isn't something to be given, traded, or thrown away. How dare they protect their virginity like it's something precious? How dare they hold their heads so high, so certain that their souls are clean, so certain that someone will love them someday, so certain that someone will earn their love?

This is my Friday night date—in the dark, forbidden—while those girls are going to movies, holding hands, first-kissing at the front door before curfew. Maybe they're in love, maybe they're holding hands with the boy they will marry. It will soon be time for that ultimate moment. They will plan the night carefully—the soft music, the flowers, the candles. He will be gentle. He will look into her eyes and ask if she wants him to stop. She will say she wants it, and she will mean it. He will say "I love you," and he will mean it. And these are real words, not just the absence of words. This is "Yes" the way "Yes" was intended.

But that is not my kind of yes. I'm the girl whose answer is her silence. I am the girl who doesn't say no. And this sounds like consent. This looks enough like wanting it. I will show up in the shower, and Jason will be waiting for me, and my mouth will never move. He will touch me and I will let him, and that will be all that I know how to say.

CHRISTOPHER

It's after community
meeting and before Group, and everybody's outside on the
patio, but I'm staying inside because my asthma's been acting
up from being around everybody smoking all the time. I'm
just waiting around, trying to hit the Ping-Pong ball against
the wall, which isn't really working too well, and guess who just
comes right up and starts talking to me? Jason. I don't think
he's ever actually talked to me. Like we've been part of the
same conversations before, but we've never directly addressed
each other. So he just walks right up and says, "Christopher,
can I talk to you?" like it's the most natural thing in the world.
Well, not really natural, because he seems pretty nervous if
you ask me, but you know what I mean.

So I'm like, "Yes?" and he starts telling me what happened last night, all whispering like I'm his best friend and he's telling me his biggest secret, and I'm trying to be a good listener even though the whole time I'm thinking, *Is this really happening?* and wondering if he's playing a trick on me. But he keeps talking, and I realize his voice sounds different from normal, like he's not making jokes or pretending he doesn't care about anything, like he actually sounds serious, and that's when I really start listening.

At first he was talking about how he's horny. To be honest, that's why I wasn't really listening at first, because I was sure it was the beginning of some mean joke where I was the punch line. I'm used to that kind of thing. Even at youth group, where you'd expect everyone to be nice and live as a model of Jesus. Well, they're not and they don't, and they still make fun of me. And Jason's talking about how being in here and not having sex has been torture and he can kind of understand why guys do the kinds of things they do in prison. And I'm like, *Hold on right there. I am not interested, thank you very much,* even though I don't say that out loud. I just kind of look at him like he's crazy and I'm a little scared of him. But he doesn't even notice. He just keeps talking, and I realize he doesn't really want to have a conversation. He just wants someone to listen, so I try to get comfortable and just listen.

He's saying something about how he was waiting in one of the shower rooms last night and freaking out because it was the least romantic place on earth, and I'm thinking, *Why would you want the shower to be romantic?* And he keeps talking about how he realized how sober he was, like really, really sober, and how it's kind of embarrassing that he's never even been with a girl without having at least a few drinks in him, and he's probably never been with a sober girl before either, and what if neither of them could remember what to do? And I'm like, "What are you talking about?" and I say it out loud this time, and he's like, "Are you even listening to me?" like I hurt his feelings, which I can tell you is a strange thing to see from Jason. So I say, "Yes, of course I'm listening."

He keeps talking about how he felt like a virgin last night, all insecure and nervous like he was going to puke, and how he knew if he just had a few beers in him he'd feel okay, just a shot or two to take the edge off and he'd feel like a man. He was just standing in there in the shower stall, waiting to have sex with a girl he didn't even know, and that bothered him for the first time in his life. That's when I realize what he's talking about, and I'm like, "Oh, Kelly!" and he's like, "Is something wrong with you, dude?" and I say, "I'm always like this," so he keeps talking.

He thought he was going to have a heart attack when he

heard Kelly open the door. Then she said, "Jason?" and he said, "Come and get it" or something equally stupid. He actually admits to sounding like a douche, which I figure means this therapy is working. Kelly wanted to turn off the lights, so it was dark, and Jason accidentally elbowed her in the ribs when she got into the shower stall, which was definitely not romantic, if you ask me. Then they started kissing, and he couldn't tell if she was kissing back, and he wondered if that's the way it's always been, if the girls have only ever been half there and he's just been too drunk to notice.

Then he starts getting graphic, talking about his hand going up her shirt, and her arms around his neck and pushing against him, and sliding his hands into the waist of her jeans, and her breath all warm and wet on his neck, and I'm like, *Why are you telling me all this?* but I don't actually say it, because I'm kind of in shock. He's talking about how he should have started feeling the electricity by then, but he was still thinking too much. That's when he noticed that Kelly's body was limp, that her arms were just hanging around his neck, that her lips were barely moving against his, just opening and closing like a fish breathing. So he asked her if she was still there, and then it felt like her body was tightening, like she was retreating, and he doesn't know what he did wrong, so I tell him, "I don't know either."

That's when he stops looking at me. It's like he's trying to get his eyes as far away from me as he can without actually turning around and leaving. He keeps talking, like I'm not even there but he has to confess to something, even if it's just to the air. He says that's when he panicked. He thought he had to do something fast or she'd change her mind. He had to act or she'd leave him. So he started unbuttoning her pants. His other hand found the back of her thigh and pulled her leg around him. It wasn't fun anymore but it felt like something he had to do. I don't tell him I'm starting to get uncomfortable. I don't tell him I'm scared of what he might say.

He says she said "Stop" when he put his hand in her pants. But he didn't stop. And she said "Stop" again. He says he remembers her straining against him. He remembers his mouth on her neck. He remembers feeling her pulse in his lips. When she said "Stop" the third time, she did it with her fists against his chest, and then he was up against the wall. He could feel the burn of her shove on his skin. He could hear her crying in the darkness. He could hear her trying to catch her breath.

He remembers feeling angry. He remembers thinking it was not him who made her cry, it was not his fault, how dare she think it was his fault. He said, "Kelly, say something." He thought, *You're pathetic. How dare you.* He said, "You fucking bitch, say something." His hands found her wrists. Then he shook her. Hard.

That's when the door opened. That's when the lights turned on. He could suddenly see her face in front of his, her pupils adjusting to the sudden light, her eyes big with fear and worry and who knows what else. He let go of her hands then. He stepped back, and she was small and cowering in the corner of the shower stall. He could not get far enough away from her. There were footsteps. There was someone breathing across the tile wall behind them.

That's when he heard the AC on night duty say, "Time's up." That's when the shower curtain was pulled open to reveal Lilana saying, "Kelly, are you really as dumb as you look? You know I check on your room every fifteen minutes. Did you *want* to get caught?"

Kelly's eyes were closed and her hands were clenched at her sides. I wonder what she was thinking then. I wonder what she wanted to say.

Lilana said, "Wait till Shirley hears about this. Boy, you're in trouble." She looked right at Jason and said, "Are you proud of yourself?" That's when he felt the knife slicing through him. Because he was not proud of himself. Not one bit.

Lilana said, "Kelly, come on." Kelly's eyes opened, but she didn't look at anything. She just said, "Sorry," and I can almost hear how her voice must have sounded, like something fragile and breaking.

Lilana said, "You think I can't tell what you were just about to let this boy do? Do you think I'm stupid?" Kelly said, "Sorry," again, and Lilana said, "You bet you are," and they walked out of the shower stall, and they were sent to their rooms to worry until the morning.

That's when Jason looks at me and says, "I'm not afraid of getting punished." He looks me right in the eyes and says, "I'm afraid of what I could have done if Lilana hadn't stopped us."

I don't know what to say, and I tell him so. All I know is that I feel like I'm looking at someone I've never met before. "So what happened?" I finally say.

"That's the weird part," he says. "Nothing happened. Shirley called us into her office this morning and said we're not allowed to be within ten feet of each other. That's all. Kelly didn't say anything." He looks down. "I almost wish she had."

We stand there for a while not talking, and it starts feeling pretty awkward. I feel like I should make a joke or something to break the silence, but for once in his life Jason doesn't look like he's in a joking mood. I open my mouth to say something stupid, but all of a sudden Jason says real quiet, like he doesn't want anyone to hear him, "I don't want to be my father." I don't know what to do, so I pat him on the back. Just a couple of pats. Then I take my hand back. I say, "You're not a monster," and he looks at me, and I swear he's almost crying, and he says, "Thank you," and I can tell he really means it.

That's when everybody starts coming inside, and just like that, Jason looks like regular old Jason again. "Time for fucking Group," he says, all normal, like this conversation never even happened. He starts heading toward the room, and I'm left standing there holding all this new information. Then I see Kelly, and she looks at me for a second, and something's definitely different about her. Then I can hear Shirley yelling at everybody to "Sit the fuck down now," and Kelly starts running toward the room, and I follow her because I don't know what else to do.

GROUP

SHIRLEY: Eva, I was hoping we could spend some time in Group today talking about you.

EVA: How about not.

SHIRLEY: Just humor me for a few minutes, Eva. Then you can go back to your silent act.

EVA: Fine. What do you want to know?

SHIRLEY: Why don't you tell us a little about your friends, school, life, and home. Anything. You pick.

EVA: I don't know. My friends are cool.

SHIRLEY: How are they cool?

EVA: They're not shallow and fake like everybody else at my school.

CHRISTOPHER: Do they do drugs?

EVA: A little. Not much, really. Not like me.

SHIRLEY: What was their reaction to you coming here?

EVA: They all came over the night before I left. They said they'd support me in any way I needed. Like they wouldn't get high around me or anything.

KELLY: Wow, you're really lucky. My friends just acted like I don't exist anymore.

SHIRLEY: What do you think about that, Eva? Do you think you're lucky?

EVA: Sure. Whatever.

SHIRLEY: It sounds to me like your friends really care about you.

EVA: I guess.

SHIRLEY: How about school? What's that like for you?

EVA: What's it like for anyone? It sucks.

SHIRLEY: Can you elaborate?

EVA: I go to class. Sometimes I do my homework. If I'm lucky, maybe I learn something. Mostly I'm just waiting for it to be over so I can graduate and get out of there.

SHIRLEY: What are your plans after you graduate?

EVA: I don't know.

SHIRLEY: Just try to imagine it.

EVA: I guess move to Seattle. Get a job making coffee, maybe. I haven't really thought that far.

SHIRLEY: Okay, that's fine. Why don't you tell us a little bit about your family?

EVA: No.

SHIRLEY: Your mother dying must have been really painful for you.

EVA: I'm done talking now.

SHIRLEY: I know this is hard.

EVA: I said I'm done.

SHIRLEY: Eva, you're only going to get as much out of this experience as you put in.

EVA: I know.

SHIRLEY: I can't force you to open up. I'm not going to try to trick you.

EVA: Okay, then.

SHIRLEY: Fine.

EVA: Fine.

PERSONAL ESSAY

OLIVIA

Did I mention that I'm not from around here? I'm from a gated community of mansions in Virginia, a quick commute to DC for my father. I could have gone to any number of high-class rehabs back home, the kind that have a revolving-door policy with the many boarding schools in the area. But my family decided that I should come here, on the other side of the country, far away from anyone who would notice.

CHRISTOPHER

There's this girl, Samantha, who I'm supposed to marry as soon as we're both eighteen. We've known each other since we were babies, her mom is friends with my mom, and she's homeschooled and just as weird as me, maybe even weirder, so it makes sense that we'd end up together. Here's the plan that's been decided for us: The summer after we finish high school, we get married. Then we both go to the state college in Pullman. Then missionary work for a couple years in a poor country. Then we move back and find a house in the same neighborhood we grew up in and start making babies. Pretty exciting, huh?

JASON

When I was ten, I beat up this kid Sammy Melber. He was in the hospital for three days. I don't even remember why I did it. He was just one of those kids, you know? The kind who are asking for it, the guy with the mom who made him lunches every day and wrote a little note on the napkin. He never did anything to me. It just felt like it was my duty to bring him down a little.

KELLY

My sisters are sick. Like, really sick. They have Down syndrome, which would be more than enough by itself, but they also have this really bad heart condition that sometimes goes with it. It'd be bad enough to have one sick sister, so imagine what it's like having two perfect little fragile angels who are constantly needing things and could die any minute. Don't get me wrong—they don't whine. No, they're too perfect for that. We can't afford vacations but we can still somehow afford to travel across the country every July for the National Down Syndrome Congress, so I can sit around a stuffy conference center while the twins run around being special and reuniting with all their best friends from the year before. There are all these meetings for kids with Down syndrome, meetings for parents of kids with Down syndrome, but there's nothing for bored sisters of kids with Down syndrome, so I basically spend the whole time sitting by the pool scamming drinks off the loser waiters. Some of them are brave enough to ask me to join them in a supply closet or walk-in fridge. And I always go, because what else am I supposed to do?

EVA

The world was perfect and then it was not. Humans are animals and they adapt. The girl was whole and then she was not.

OLIVIA

This morning I got a card from my grandmother that said "Good luck at the new school," so I've surmised that I'm supposed to be in an exchange program with an imaginary private school that just happens to share its name and address with an adolescent rehab facility on the outskirts of Seattle.

CHRISTOPHER

I've known Samantha my whole life, but I don't know what her middle name is. Or her favorite food, or her favorite book, movie, song, what she thinks about when she's alone. And the sad thing is that I don't really care.

KELLY

My parents let me stay home from the convention this year. I somehow convinced them I was mature enough. They keep trusting me, even after I get in trouble a million times a million different ways, even after I come home way after curfew every weekend with another lame excuse, even though they must smell the alcohol on me and they must notice my bloodshot eyes night after night after night. They came home after their weekend of healing at the convention to a trashed house with shit stolen and a couple passed out in their bed. And what do they do? Do they yell and scream and throw shit? No. They send the twins to their room, make us all a cup of tea, sit me down, and say, "Honey, what's going on? Are you okay? What do you need from us?" Seriously? Who fucking does that? I wish they would just scream, even hit me—anything would be better. Because at least I could scream back. But all I can do is say I'm sorry. All I can do is clean up the mess and wait for the next one.

KELLY

I don't know why Shirley

was so easy on us. I don't know what I expected her to do, but we deserve more of a punishment than just having to stay ten feet away from each other. To be honest, the fact that I don't have to deal with Jason is a relief more than anything, like I'm getting a break from being me. But why did Shirley have to be so kind? Why didn't she scream and call me a slut like I deserve? Why didn't she bring it up in Group and humiliate me in front of everyone? It's not like her at all.

Jason won't even look at me now. It's like I don't exist anymore, like I'm nothing to him. But that's what I get for being a tease, right? That's what I get for being stupid like I always am, for laughing at all his dumb jokes, for pretending

I like him, for kissing him back, for letting him put his hands wherever he wanted, for letting him think I'd do anything he tried. But that's what I always do. Because doing what guys want is easier than anything else. Letting them have their way is easier than saying no. It's like I can just flip on a switch and suddenly I'm on autopilot. My body knows all the right moves, but I feel nothing. That way, they get what they want, and I'm numb, and everyone's happy.

It has always been so easy. I just get as drunk and as high as possible, close my eyes, and do what I'm supposed to do. The only thing I can feel is the warmth of the alcohol and coke in my blood. I feel the warmth of him wanting me—even though it's not really me, even though it's just my body—and that's usually enough. I don't need much when I'm drunk and high. That's the beauty of it. I don't need love or self-respect. I don't need you to care about me or how I feel. You could be anyone and it wouldn't matter. I cannot feel you or what you do to me. That's how it's supposed to go. That's what I've gotten used to.

But I was sober, and that bathroom was cold. I opened the door and the light was bright and I knew he was there behind the tile wall. The smell of cleanser was sharp in my nose. I did not want to see him. I did not want him looking at me. Suddenly nothing felt right in my body. I could feel too much.

I could feel myself not wanting to be there. But I could feel him there wanting me, and I knew what I had to do. So even though everything inside was telling me to turn the other way and run out that door, I tried to be with him. He has to know I tried. But it was like there were voices inside me telling me to do something else, like they had been there all along but I'd always been too drunk to hear them. And when he touched me, they were screaming. They said "Stop," but my mouth couldn't. They said "No," but my body tried to follow his. The more he touched me, the louder they got, until it was too hard to kiss him back, until it was too hard to pretend.

There was something else too. There was more than Jason and me in that room. There were memories like blurry images in the darkness, shades of gray and shapes that looked like people. I felt the pressure of him against me, but the air around us changed, became thick like smoke suffocating, and we were replaced by ghosts. When I reached for him, I lifted the arms of a girl who resembled me but was not me, a girl with eyes filled with terror. And the taste in my mouth was not him, it was only the shadows of him, it was a dusty basement four years ago, it was vodka and orange juice and a girl who had no idea what she was getting into. And then it was not Jason in that bathroom with me. It was that older boy four years ago, and it was not the fuzzy maybe memory. It was suddenly sharp and hot and fiercely in focus. And it was not fine, okay, no problem, numb—No, it was not any of those things I wanted to believe it had been.

Because some things are stronger than vodka and orange juice. Some things like pain and fear and ripping apart. And his hands like stains on my body. And his violence so cruel inside me. Jason, it was not you, but it was all of you. It was all you boys and men who never even had to ask. It was all you boys who took me. Because I gave myself away like I was worth nothing. Because if I *let* you have me, you couldn't take me like he did, couldn't hurt me like he did.

Chris Henderson. I remember. You hurt me. I did not say yes.

I can taste the memory of vodka and orange juice. I can taste you sour in my mouth. I can taste the pain, still raw, still fresh, released from its hiding place, swarming around in truth like torture, and there is no sending it back.

DRUG & ALCOHOL HISTORY QUESTIONNAIRE

QUESTION #4:

Have you ever tried to stop or cut down on your own?
What happened?

I made a schedule. I planned how many pills I
would take each day. But I could never follow it for
long. I always needed more.

I've never tried to quit. Why would I want to quit?

I told myself I wouldn't drink until the weekend.

I said I'd take a break for a month.

I said I'd take a break for a week.

I said I'd take a break for two days.

I promised myself I wouldn't get wasted.
I'd only have a couple drinks.
I wouldn't lose control.

I woke up every morning and promised myself I
wouldn't smoke that day.

I didn't want to quit. I just wanted to stop for a
couple weeks so I could get my tolerance back.

I just wanted it to be like it was at the beginning.

What are you supposed to do when you forget
what normal feels like?

Somehow those drinks always made it into my
hand and into my mouth.
Somehow they kept coming and coming and there
was nothing I could do about it.

I promised God this time would be the last time.

Imagine wanting something you hate.

God, what's wrong with me?

I was able to quit for two weeks once, but it felt
like torture.
It felt like I was holding my breath the whole
time.

My hands were shaking.
I couldn't sleep.
I couldn't eat.

This isn't normal.
This isn't the way normal people live.

I tried to switch to beer. I thought it couldn't get
me into trouble. But I kept drinking until it did. I
kept drinking until I didn't care about the promise
I'd made, and it wasn't long until I was back to
everything else, and it was even worse than before.

Normal people don't need to get high every day.

Normal people can go a week without drinking.

Normal people can keep promises they make to
themselves.

Imagine an obsession so strong you can't think
about anything else.
Imagine starvation.
Now imagine something worse.

I can't remember what it feels like to not need to
drink.

I don't know how many times I tried to control
it. I told myself only on weekends, only at night,
only at parties, never alone, never at school,
never while babysitting, never while driving. I'd
be able to do it for a while, but things would
always fall apart.

I couldn't do anything but sleep and eat.

You get to a certain point and it's not you making the decisions anymore.

You get to a certain point and there's no turning back.

I needed it to feel normal.

I had no choice.

I wanted to die.

I tried, but I just needed to make the pain stop. It was the only thing that I knew would make the pain stop.

I always meant it. Every single time. I always planned to keep those promises.

You can only fail so many times.

I thought one beer couldn't hurt. But that one beer turned to three, then five, then eight, then it was back to the coke, then I don't remember.

I am not normal.

I will never be normal.

It's like I'm possessed, like there's this demon inside me and as soon as it gets a taste of what it wants, it takes over. It's like the other part of me disappears, the part of me that wants to be good, and there's nothing left but this demon on a rampage, and the good part of me just hides and tries to stay out of the way.

Imagine everything feeling wrong.
Imagine a hole in your chest the size of God.

Nothing else mattered.
All I could think about was getting high.

Imagine trying to live without air.
Now imagine something worse.

CHRISTOPHER

Today's a big day.

There's about to be a major news announcement. Everybody's been buzzing since before breakfast with rumors about something exciting that happened last night, and apparently I slept through the whole thing. I guess I'm the only one who actually sleeps in this place. I've been trying to catch up all morning, but there are so many weird theories floating around. The various clues have led me to believe the events in question involved some kind of contraband, the Heroin Addict, and/or the Satan Worshipper. We're all sitting here on the edge of our seats, waiting for community meeting to start, watching Ponytail AC's face for any kind of clue about what to expect, but he's just standing against the wall like he's trying to be invisible, and his eyes are all sketchy, darting back and forth. All the ACs have this same look of fear in their eyes to varying degrees, like they're waiting for us to erupt in some kind of *Lord of the Flies* mutiny. Except for Lilana, of course. She's the only one who's never impressed by anything we do.

One of the counselors from another Group walks in, and Ponytail immediately relaxes. I guess it must be a huge relief to not have to be responsible for a room full of teenage drug addicts anymore. Really, we could turn on him at any second. I'd be scared too. The counselor in charge looks like he could protect him, though. He's a big guy with tattoos and a big deep voice, and if anyone can protect Ponytail from us, it's probably him, and maybe Lilana. As soon as he stands up there, everyone calms down and looks straight at him, and I swear it's the best behaved we've ever been. If someone walked in right now, they'd probably think we were some kind of honors class instead of a bunch of criminals.

"Good morning, everyone," the Buff Counselor says in his gravelly voice, and I hear the Pregnant Girl whisper to her friend, "He is so cute," and then they both giggle, but I think he looks like one of those wrestlers on TV, the fake ones who are always yelling and pounding their shaved chests with their fists, and I honestly don't see what's so cute about that, but of course I'm no expert on what girls think is cute.

Buff Counselor says, "We're going to skip introductions this morning if that's okay with you guys. We have a lot to cover and no one new is joining us today."

No one objects, but I bet Compulsive Liar is secretly fuming because everybody knows he loves listing off in front of an audience every morning all the drugs he pretends he's addicted to. Everyone's always making fun of him and calling him crazy behind his back, but I can kind of understand how someone would end up that way. I mean, if no one ever pays attention to you telling the truth, then it probably makes sense to try lying for a change.

Eva leans over and says into my ear, "I heard they found needles in the Heroin Addict's room." Then Kelly leans over on the other side of me and says, "No, it's worse. They found him OD'd on the floor of the bathroom." Then Eva says, "Someone on the outside snuck a baggie through the patio fence." Then Kelly says, "It was his girlfriend." Eva says, "He has a girlfriend?" And I'm happy for them that they're getting along, but I'd prefer it if they found another way to communicate than through my head.

"I know there are a lot of rumors circulating this morning about events that occurred last night," Buff Counselor says. "There are some things I can't share with you, but I can tell you that, as of last night, Erik Vine is no longer a member of our community."

"I knew it," says Eva. Then Kelly says, "His name was Erik?" and everyone's talking all over the place, and I must admit it is pretty exciting compared to the usual community meeting where we go around in a circle introducing ourselves for the five-millionth time.

Jason's all the way over on the other side of the room because I guess Kelly got custody of me and Eva in the separation. He's been moping around for the last couple of days, but she's gone the exact opposite direction. Nobody's said anything about it out loud, but it's kind of drastic how much she's changed. I have to say I think she's a lot prettier au naturel, but that could just be my own personal beauty aesthetic. Also, I think she looks a lot nicer without makeup, like, less mean and scary, not that she was ever particularly mean and scary, but she definitely belonged in the intimidating category. She's also dressing differently now, less sexy and grown-up and more like the girls I'm used to. It's like all of a sudden she decided to not try so hard anymore.

The weirdest thing isn't that she's in jeans and a sweatshirt, or even that she's talking to Eva; it's something else completely, but I can't really explain it. It's not one thing in particular like a specific behavior. It's more like a general feeling, like something new you feel when you're around her, like now you're not as sad anymore, not as weighed down. It's crazy how just being next to someone can change your feelings like that. It's like Kelly likes herself better without all that makeup.

Buff Counselor is fighting off everybody's questions now as people try to get to the bottom of things. Someone asks if he's going to jail, and someone else asks if he OD'd in the bathroom, and someone asks if he escaped, and someone says, "Who's Erik Vine?" and someone answers, "The Heroin Addict." And the other someone says, "Oh." Buff Counselor isn't saying anything; he's just standing up there like a big silent rock while Ponytail looks more nervous the louder and more unruly the crowd gets.

The rest of the Scary Guys might know something, but Gas Man left yesterday for a high-security boarding school in the Arizona desert, and I don't know anyone brave or stupid enough to talk to the other two. Buff Counselor says, "It became clear that Erik did not belong in a community of recovery. That's all I'm going to say." Could he be any more mysterious? It's like he wants to torture us. The crowd is obviously not satisfied with the answer, but they calm down because Buff Counselor gives the impression that there's no hope of getting anything more out of him, and the excitement in the room is replaced by disappointment.

Just when it seems we're sufficiently settled down and ready to move on, Hippie Girl raises her hand and says, "I have something I'd like to bring up with the community." I have no idea what she's talking about, but I can see her Group members rolling their eyes and looking at each other, and even though she's really annoying and always hanging on to Eva, I kind of feel sorry for her to be that disliked by her own Group.

"Yes, Sophie?" Buff Counselor says, and Kelly goes, "Her name's Sophie?" and Eva nods, and I realize I didn't even know that even though I'm around her all the time and she introduces herself at community meeting every day.

Sophie says, "I would like to discuss the censorship of nontraditional religious books and how basically it's against the Constitution that you took away . . . that guy . . . um . . ."

"Yes, Sophie?" says Buff Counselor.

"Um, *his* books," she says, pointing at Satan Worshipper. He smiles a wicked grin, and I swear his teeth are black.

Now that I think of it, does anyone know anyone's name in here? Are we really that self-absorbed?

Buff Counselor says, "I believe this matter has already been settled between Shawn and his counselor, and if I'm not mistaken, it doesn't involve you, does it, Sophie?"

"It does involve me if it involves another human being's goddess-given rights to free speech," she says, and the whole room groans in unison, even Ponytail, and it's actually quite a lovely sound, like we're the Rehab Tabernacle Choir or something. Sophie the Hippie is always trying to protest something, which I find kind of endearing, but which makes Eva want to kill her. But it's nice to see someone care about something, you know? First was the use of Styrofoam cups for tea, then something about genetically modified meat in our lunches, which shouldn't really concern her since, of course, she's vegan.

This time Eva leans over and whispers, "Someone finally complained about his Satan worshipper books, so they took them away," and Kelly says, "It's about time," and I wonder when they decided to become best friends, because last time I checked, they didn't even talk to each other. Maybe Eva decided she'd be nice after Kelly stopped showing off her boobs. But who knows how girls think?

Buff Counselor says, "The administration decided that the books were a distraction and not appropriate for this environment, and Shawn willingly agreed to let us keep them for him until he goes home."

Eva says, "I bet we're going to see him on the news in a couple months for blowing up his school," and Kelly says, "Totally."

"But you have no right to decide what religion is

appropriate for someone else," Sophie says, and her voice is even whinier and more desperate than usual. Someone throws a wadded-up piece of paper at her, and Satan Worshipper is just sitting over there laughing like a maniac, and people are starting to get restless, and Kelly says, "How embarrassing," and Eva says, "She probably thinks he lights candles under a full moon and casts spells for a bountiful harvest." Then they're both laughing like crazy, and now the whole room is laughing. Buff Counselor says, "Okay. Time for Group," like Sophie isn't even there, and everybody gets up and starts walking to their rooms. Sophie's just standing there with her mouth hanging open, and it just amazes me how many ways there are to humiliate someone.

GROUP

SHIRLEY: Eva, let's talk about your mother's death.

EVA: Let's not.

SHIRLEY: It's obviously had a huge impact on your life. Don't you think it's a good idea to address it?

EVA: I don't need to. I've talked about it enough with all the shrinks my dad sent me to. It's over. She's gone. End of story. Can't you just read my essays or something?

SHIRLEY: What does the Group think?

JASON: Bullshit.

KELLY: Bullshit.

CHRISTOPHER: It sounds like you're still really angry.

EVA: Jesus, you people drive me crazy.

SHIRLEY: How do you feel about what Christopher said? Do you think you're angry?

EVA: Of course I'm angry. Wouldn't you be? When she died, it just gave my dad permission to forget about me, so basically I lost two parents at the same time. That's a lot for a kid to deal with.

SHIRLEY: But you said yourself that he got you counseling. Can you give him some credit for that, at least?

EVA: All that proves is that he wanted to hand me off to someone else and let them deal with me.

KELLY: Do you blame him for your drug use?

EVA: Do you think you're the counselor now, Kelly?

SHIRLEY: It's a good question, Eva. Do you hold your dad responsible for your addiction?

EVA: It probably wouldn't have gotten so bad if he'd been paying closer attention.

SHIRLEY: So you blame him for not catching you sooner? That's a big responsibility to put on him, don't you think?

EVA: Jesus, Shirley, whose side are you on?

SHIRLEY: What do you guys think? Do you think she's being too hard on her dad?

CHRISTOPHER: Maybe.

OLIVIA: Yes.

KELLY: She hasn't talked a whole lot about him, or about anything, really, so it's hard to tell.

EVA: You want to know what it was like after my mom died?

KELLY: It might help us understand better.

EVA: There's nothing to understand. Before she died, we were a family. We were happy. Then she got sick and everything fell apart. It was my dad's job to keep it together. It was his job to stay strong for us, but he didn't. He was selfish. He let things fall apart. He didn't even think about what I was going through.

KELLY: Eva, it's not his fault that she died.

EVA: Shut the fuck up.

CHRISTOPHER: We're just trying to help.

EVA: None of you have any idea what you're talking about. None of you know what it's like to lose your mother.

JASON: Maybe *you* don't know what it's like to lose your wife.

EVA: What?

SHIRLEY: Jason, how nice of you to join us.

JASON: No problem.

SHIRLEY: Care to elaborate?

JASON: She's sitting here complaining about how her father let her down and how she was going through all this pain, but did she ever stop to think what he must have been going through? Eva wasn't the only one who lost someone. I mean, he just lost the person he thought he was going to spend the rest of his life with, and you expect him to be all strong and take care of this kid by himself? Cut the man a little slack.

EVA: Fuck you, Jason.

KELLY: He does have a point.

EVA: Fuck you, too.

KELLY: He could have probably said it a little nicer, but you have to admit it's true. Your dad had his own shit to go through.

EVA: Fuck you. Fuck all of you. Why are you on his side all of a sudden? What about me? Why doesn't anyone care about me?

CHRISTOPHER: It's okay, Eva.

EVA: No, it's not.

SHIRLEY: Take a tissue.

EVA: I don't want your fucking tissues, Shirley.

OLIVIA: Can I say something?

JASON: Behold, she speaks.

KELLY: Shut up, Jason.

SHIRLEY: Eva, is it okay if Olivia says something?

EVA: Sure, whatever. Knock yourself out.

OLIVIA: I know how everyone thinks I'm a snob, and you're probably right. And I know this is going to sound really harsh, but I don't know how else to say it. Just take it from someone who knows—Eva, you're kind of acting like a spoiled brat.

EVA: Excuse me?

OLIVIA: It sucks that your mom died, and I feel for you. But I've just been sitting here this whole time listening to you and thinking what I wouldn't give to have a mother like yours for just a second, and you had her for what—fourteen, fifteen years? She's gone, but at least you knew what it felt like for her to love you. Believe me, I'd trade with you in a second. I'd much rather have a dead mother who loved me than a live one who doesn't.

CHRISTOPHER: You don't think your mother loves you?

OLIVIA: I know she doesn't.

CHRISTOPHER: Not even a little bit?

OLIVIA: No.

CHRISTOPHER: That can't be true. It just can't. How can a mother not love her own kid?

OLIVIA: I've been wondering that my whole life.

SHIRLEY: Eva, how do you feel about what Olivia just said?

CHRISTOPHER: Eva?

KELLY: Eva, are you okay?

EVA: I just want her back.

SHIRLEY: I know.

EVA: I just really want her back.

CHRISTOPHER: Oh, Eva.

SHIRLEY: Just let it out, sweetie.

KELLY: It's okay, Eva. We're all here for you.

SHIRLEY: Here, honey, take a tissue.

EVA: Fine.

PERSONAL ESSAY

CHRISTOPHER

You're probably wondering how I ended up here if I'm such a sheltered homeschooled kid. I'm still wondering the same thing. I mean, I never even knew places like this existed. Up until a year ago, I hardly even knew drugs existed.

EVA

This was no longer the neighborhood with the crayon-drawn houses, the smiley-face windows so inviting. No more sunshine or whispering grass. No more sandboxes. No more little girl stick figure. No more little girl. Where there once was a heart, there was now an almost-life plucked out, the size of a pecan. There was now a tiny, little death.

A gaping nowhere. Another wasteland to be filled. Just desert. Tundra. Lifeless and windburned. Just the pieces of a life that needed refitting.

OLIVIA

It's not like I was fat. I was just a regular girl, really. I know this because I've spent my life comparing myself to everyone around me. I've made it an art form. I've developed detailed systems to calculate where I stand, based on GPA, body mass index, fashion, popularity, family income, etc. Based on this criteria, I have always fared somewhere in the safe middle. What I lack in popularity, I make up for in family income. What I lack in BMI, I make up for with designer clothes.

KELLY

I was not always like this. I remember how excited I was when the twins were born. I remember going to sleep every night thinking about what a great sister I'd be, how much I'd teach them and take care of them, how we'd be best friends. And it was like that for a while. I remember when they came home from the hospital. I was constantly asking Mom if I could help, if I could hold them, feed them, change their diapers. When there was nothing for me to do, I'd make up chores just so I could be around them.

JASON

Oh, this is a good one. You're going to like this one, Shirley. When I was twelve, on my birthday, Dad took me to this fancy hotel room. There was a lady in the bedroom, lying on the bed in her underwear. I remember her saying, "Happy Birthday, Jason. Your father's told me so much about you." And I remember wanting to get out of there so bad, wanting to get away from this woman my dad knew well enough to tell about me, this practically naked woman that was talking to me like a teacher would, except she was naked and sexy.

OLIVIA

You must understand that there are calculations for everything. Even the most abstract concept can be rated on a scale of one to ten. For instance:

Kelly—Beauty: 8.5

Jason—Class: 2

Christopher—Confidence: 3

Eva—Bitchiness: 7

Me—Perfection: a big fat 0

You may think this is weird, but really—what's so strange about trying to make sense of the world?

CHRISTOPHER

Part of me still thinks I'm the good kid I've always been, that I've never really done drugs, not really, like this is a nightmare and I'll wake up soon and be just like I was before—before Todd started climbing into my bedroom, before his coke and his meth and all the secrets that came with him.

JASON

I knew my dad had fucked her. I knew it as he stood there so proudly, like there was nothing weird about any of this. And he said, "Son, I'll be in the other room. Happy birthday." Then he winked. He fucking winked. Then he closed the door behind him and I was alone in a hotel room with a woman my father had fucked.

EVA

You'd expect something like a green sprout, perhaps a leaf unfurling in stop-motion photography. Something reaching to the sun. Something hopeful with its timid chlorophyll. But the girl's rebirth was more like a fungus. Something flat and spreading and sinister. Without color. Without much need for light. Something meant to live in caves. Under rotting wood. Hidden. And someone said, "Rapunzel, Rapunzel, let down your hair." So the girl cut it off. And the rain said, "Look what happens when you are seen." So the girl dressed herself in rags.

KELLY

I'd look at my sisters sleeping, run my finger across the soft down on their heads, wedge my finger inside their tiny little fists and pretend they were holding tight and knew it was me.

OLIVIA

There are scales and numbers and grades and categories. Then there is plain old organization: checklists, to-do lists, files, systems, and on and on. When eveything's in its place, the world seems a little less crazy. When my books are alphabetized and perfectly straight on my bookshelf, I can breathe easier. When my sheets are bound tight to my bed, the pillows all set up according to their invisible grid, my alarm clock and lamp balanced on my bedside table—only then can I leave my room in the morning. Mother says I should let the maid do the tidying, but she doesn't get it. She doesn't get anything. She's too immersed in her social theatrics. She's too distracted by her pills and martini cocktails.

CHRISTOPHER

Part of me thinks I'll wake up and still be that same sheltered homeschooled kid, and life will be uncomplicated, and there will be no more need for secrets. But once something like this happens, there's no going back to the way things used to be. I may be naive, but I know that much.

JASON

It's not like I was inexperienced. I was twelve, but I'd had Loraine McClellan suck my cock a few times. It's not like I wasn't ready for sex or anything. I don't know what it was—my dad in the other room, the fact that she was a whore, the fact that he had fucked her—it could have been anything. But I couldn't get it up. There she was with her black lace lingerie and big tits and everything, but I didn't want to fuck her. I wanted to run out of that room and never come back. And she was all, "Oh, honey, what's wrong? Oh, I guess you're not quite a man yet," and I wanted to kill her. I seriously wanted to hurt her, but I felt so fucking small. Do you have any idea how that feels? To be a man and feel inferior to a fucking whore?

EVA

There were caves with welcome signs. There were creatures that did not mind the girl's cavity full of fungus, or the rags, or the mealy white scalp, or the newly gray tint of her skin. They were huddled around a fire. They were dressed in black. They said, "Join us." They said, "We are as lost as you are." The fire remembered. It said, "Let me cleanse you." It said, "Let me take away everything you have collected."

KELLY

I remember feeling a warmth inside my chest, a pressure like wet sand. And I was such a dumb kid that I was convinced it was God holding my heart.

CHRISTOPHER

Sometimes this place

isn't too bad. Like today, everybody who's been on their best behavior and doesn't have any demerits gets special activity privileges to be released into the real world. It's exciting when we get to go anywhere, but usually it's just to a meeting in a church basement full of people just like us except older. Either that or it's the abandoned playground across the street, which is kind of depressing, in my opinion. But today they're actually letting us out in public. I'm so excited I can hardly think straight, because guess where they're taking us? Bowling! We're going to an actual bowling alley where we're going to be around normal people and rent shoes and everything.

Eva's been freaking out because this New Guy arrived a

couple days ago and she thinks she's in love with him. She looked at me all serious at breakfast and was like "I thought my heart was cold, Christopher. I thought I'd never love again," and I swear it took all my strength to not laugh in her face. I know that's mean, but really, who says stuff like that besides people in the cheesy Lifetime movies my mom watches?

The New Guy is a heroin addict, but he's not scary like the old one. He actually seems like a pretty nice guy, even though he wears an army jacket that's too big for him, even indoors, and he's always talking about how he wants to join the army as soon as he turns eighteen. It is totally out of character for Eva to like a guy like this, but she says they have a bond because they're both opiate addicts and have to take the same medicine so they don't get sick. He was in some other place before this one, and because of his good behavior there they're letting him have all the activity privileges here right away, which isn't fair at all, if you ask me. I've had good behavior my whole life, but I had to wait a whole week like everyone else before they let me go anywhere. He and Eva had some kind of special appointment yesterday with the doctor that only opiate addicts were invited to, but the doctor was late, so they spent a whole hour waiting in his office, just the two of them. Eva got all googly-eyed when she told me about his rough life and how strong and brave he's been to survive it, and I wonder what makes him so much more special than the rest of us. Does being a heroin addict automatically put him on the top of the drug addict pyramid? He's just a skinny guy in an army jacket, as far as I'm concerned. The fact that he has track marks and was homeless for a few weeks doesn't impress me one bit.

They're supposed to be on my bowling team, but they're all lovey-dovey and totally ignoring me so I'm just going to talk to Olivia and Kelly, who are on the lane next to us. Jason's on the farthest lane away, and I have to admit I kind of miss him hanging around and making fun of everyone. I guess Eva and the New Guy are the new rehab It Couple now, which is just bizarre.

Everyone in the bowling alley seems totally afraid of us, which is pretty funny. I was on my way to the bathroom and this lady whipped her arm out to shield her daughter when I walked by, like I was going to attack her or something. It doesn't help that everyone's being overly obnoxious on purpose. One guy stood on top of a chair and announced where we're from, so please don't give us any drugs or alcohol, thank you very much. Another guy started scratching himself all over and bugging his eyes out and moaning about needing a fix. The Pregnant Girl stuck her belly out and started talking real loud about needing to get a paternity test to see which one of her five boyfriends is the babydaddy. Seriously, you can't take us anywhere.

After Olivia got over the initial shock of having to wear used shoes and to put her fingers into dirty bowling ball holes, she actually seems to be having a good time. She's not laughing, or even really smiling for that matter, but the fact that she's participating and not scowling at everyone shows real progress. Kelly even convinced her to sit with us at meals instead of by herself at the end of the table like she'd been doing. She doesn't talk much, but at least now she's starting to seem somewhat human. She's on some new medicine for obsessive-compulsive disorder, and it looks like it's working, because Kelly says she's stopped doing so much of her crazy organizing. She still doesn't eat, though. She gets a plate of food like she's supposed to, but mostly what she does is push it around. Sometimes she'll take bites, but half the time she just spits it out into her napkin. I don't know if anyone else is paying attention or notices this kind of thing, and I know I'm supposed to tell someone, but it just doesn't seem right somehow. It seems to me like what Olivia really needs is to learn how to trust people, and that's never going to happen if we tattle on her.

All Olivia's bowled so far are gutter balls, but she seems almost proud of them. Shirley told her that bowling would be a good opportunity to practice becoming comfortable with failure, and I think Olivia's actually enjoying it. Every gutter ball seems to take some of her anxiety with it. Surprisingly, I'm one of the best bowlers here, which I know isn't that big a deal, but it still makes me feel kind of proud. I don't have a whole lot of competition, that's for sure. One of the girls accidentally ripped her fake fingernail off, and someone else dropped a ball onto his foot. But no one really seems to care that we suck, because we're all too busy being happy to be outside and doing something normal for once. After everyone got tired of trying to scare the Normies, I think we actually started to resemble real teenagers. If you walked into the bowling alley right now, you might not even notice us. You might think we're just here for someone's birthday party, that any second someone's mom is going to bring out a cake and we're going to sing "Happy Birthday" totally out of tune, and whoever's birthday it is will blow out the candles and make a wish for something normal like getting into a good college. We can only wish to someday make wishes like that. For now I'd say we're doing pretty well just making it through the day without having a meltdown and running out of this place screaming.

The New Guy has to go to the bathroom, so suddenly Eva wants to be my friend again. She comes over and hooks her arm around mine and says, "Oh my God. I am so in love," and I try not to show how happy I am that she's talking to me again, or how mad I am that she wasn't. Those are already strange feelings to have at the same time, plus there's a third one that I can't quite explain, like there's this thing in my stomach burning and threatening to come out, and all I can think about is me being the friend she can tell these kinds of things to but never being the one who gets to tell them. Even miserable Eva gets her chance at love. But not me. Never me. I don't get a chance to tell anyone anything like that.

She's pulling on my arm and explaining how the New Guy is unlike anyone she's met before, like, "totally authentic," which I take to imply that I am something less than totally authentic, so I'm like, "What about the army jacket? What's so authentic about that?" She gets this look on her face like she's glad I finally asked, and she starts talking some nonsense about a moment of clarity and a sign from God, so I tell her she's starting to sound like the Jesus freaks I go to church with. Just then, the New Guy comes back from the bathroom, and Eva tells him to tell the story about how he got sober and why he wants to join the army. Olivia and Kelly just finished their game, so they come over too, and now all of a sudden it's like he's surrounded by a bunch of groupies, and I'm getting more depressed by the second.

The girls get all sad when he talks about his mom kicking him out of the house. They're practically crying by the time he gets to the part about getting strung out on heroin and living in a park with a bunch of junkies and being scared of getting jumped all the time. I have to admit it is a pretty impressive story, and he does seem like a sensitive guy, so it's getting pretty hard for me to keep hating him. I look at Eva, and she's practically glowing, she's so happy, and I feel a little squeeze in my stomach like jealousy or sadness, but also like I know she deserves to be happy and care about somebody for once, so I decide to get over myself and just try to like this guy like everyone else does, because that's the Christian thing to do.

He's at the part in the story where he's really strung out and hasn't showered for weeks and doesn't know the last time he ate. Everyone's leaning in to listen, and it's almost like we're not in the middle of a bowling alley with loud country music playing and balls and pins crashing all over the place. He's almost whispering when he says, "I probably weighed about eighty pounds, I was so sick. I remember just sitting there under the freeway on an old flea-infested mattress, listening to the cars driving over me, and I decided that as soon as I got up enough strength I was going to climb up there and jump in front of those cars, because there was no point in living anymore if I was going to keep living like that." I can see tears welling up in Eva's eyes, and it sounds like everyone else has stopped breathing.

"But just then my phone starts ringing, so I answer it," the New Guy says. I look around, and no one else seems surprised by a homeless kid having a cell phone. "It's this army recruiter that came to my high school months ago, before I dropped out. I don't remember giving anyone my number, but here was this guy calling me. I never felt so lonely in my life as I did right then, and all of a sudden here's this total stranger on the phone asking how I'm doing, and for some reason I decide to tell him everything. I tell him about the drugs and the stealing and the living on the streets. I tell him about the bruises all over my veins, and how I miss my mom and my little sister. He just listens and doesn't say anything, and after I've told him everything and I'm just sitting there crying into the phone, he tells me if I can live through that, then I can do anything. Then he says that the army can teach me how to respect myself again, and he talked to me for a half an hour about my future. No one's ever done anything like that for me, not even my own mother. And here's this guy I barely remember meeting, telling me he believes in me.

"And that's when I knew what I had to do. So I caught the bus to my mom's house and told her I was done and I wanted help. Now I'm here and I'm going to get sober and get my GED. Then I'm going to join the army and they're going to pay for me to go to college someday. And I know this is what I'm meant to do, that there's a reason the recruiter called me and offered me a new life just as I was about to kill myself. I owe it to him. I've never believed in God before, but something happened that day. Maybe it was just a coincidence, but whatever it was, it saved my life."

All the girls look like they either want to cradle him or rip his clothes off, and all of this goodness, all of his faith and trust and hope for the future, something about it is making me extra aware of the edge I've been feeling the last couple of days. I've been feeling a little off, like maybe there's something lurking beneath the surface, like maybe there's someone here besides the sweet innocent Christopher everybody knows, and maybe it's about time for him to come out. I don't know what it is, but the longer I'm in rehab, the more it grows. This thing that's always been inside and hidden deep is getting bigger and stronger and threatening to show itself, and I want to stop it but I also don't, and I don't know if I'm ready, but I think maybe I want what's inside turned outside, maybe I want everything out in the open, all my secrets laid out for everyone to see. I wonder what that would look like. I wonder what kind of mess it would make. I wonder if you can ever really be ready for the part of you that you've been hiding your whole life to finally come out.

There's some commotion, and the crowd of New Guy worshippers disappears. Everyone's rushing to turn their bowling shoes in because Lilana is screaming that it's time to go back. The rest of the bowling alley is watching us with one of three looks on their faces: disgusted, mesmerized, or horrified, and everyone's keeping their distance. Kelly runs up and says someone got caught drinking a beer they stole from a Normie bowler when he wasn't looking, so now we all have to get punished and go home early. You can tell everybody's pretty depressed about it because no one's laughing or making fun of anybody, and just like that, our one big chance to feel normal is gone.

KELLY

Everybody's been acting weird lately, like we're all about to simultaneously start our periods. Even Christopher's been cranky, which is totally out of character, because you're supposed to be able to always count on him to give you some hope in the future of humanity. Jason's gotten quiet and reclusive, Olivia's talking, Eva's happy, and I don't know what I am, but I know that I'm different. It's like there's been this big shift, like something's clicked, and we all found this different version of ourselves we didn't know existed. And I guess that's a good thing. I just wish it didn't feel so fucking weird.

I called my mom and asked her to send me the school assignments I've missed while I've been in here, so now I have this pile of three weeks' worth of homework to do. As soon as I opened the package, I immediately regretted it and wanted to send it all back. I remembered why it was so much easier not to care. I was sitting on my bed with all the books and work sheets spread around me, and Lilana was yelling at me to put it away until study hour, and I felt like tearing it all up or throwing it out the window, and I wanted a drink so bad I thought the feeling was going to kill me, this feeling of being stuck and a failure and hating myself and afraid all at once. I was trying to breathe like Shirley taught us to do, trying to tell myself the feeling would pass, but I didn't believe it, I just couldn't believe it. The only thing I believed was that a drink would fix it. A drink and a line would make the feeling go away. At that moment that was the only thing that was true.

I must have been crying, because Olivia came over and sat next to me and put her arm around me, and I didn't even stop to think how weird it was that she was doing that. I just felt grateful, and her arm felt strong around me even though it was so skinny and brittle. That was this morning, and now it's study hour, and I don't know if I'm going to ever finish everything I'm supposed to, but I'm going to try, and that has to be enough. Olivia said she'd help me, and when I asked her why, she said, "Isn't that what friends do?" and I said, "I have no idea," and we laughed a long time about that. She has a nice laugh. You wouldn't know by looking at her, but when she laughs, it sounds like something she was meant to do.

I don't feel great, but I don't feel terrible, either, and I guess that's how normal people feel most of the time. They live in the space between black and white, and their ups and downs are various shades of gray, not the extreme highs and lows I've always thought of as normal. I think that's one of the major differences between us and them, between addicts and Normies. Somewhere along the line we got stuck on this roller coaster that only knows how to go to the highest up and the lowest low. We get high so we can feel invincible and perfect, but the feeling never lasts. Gravity always wins, and we fall fast, to a place lower and darker than many people will probably ever know. And the crazy thing is that this is just normal for us. We cycle through these extremes all the time, and it's become as natural as breathing. Exhausting, but natural.

We've forgotten what it looks like in the middle, but I'm guessing it looks something like this—sitting in a quiet room trying to do homework and wondering what's for dinner. Simple. Nothing too exciting. Part of me feels relieved, but part of me also feels bored, like I have no idea what to do with myself, and I'm having a hard time sitting still in this chair. Part of me wants to get up and scream and tear my hair out, and part of me wants to lie down and curl up into a ball and fall asleep. And it's making me anxious. Shirley says it passes, and I want to believe her. I want to believe that someday I'll be able to sit in a chair without wanting to pull my hair out. Someday I'll be able to concentrate on what I'm doing without having to look around the room every thirty seconds. Someday sitting still and being in my skin won't feel like torture.

I think we're all feeling a little bit crazy. This is probably the longest any of us has been sober since we started using. Jason won't stop tapping his pencil on his desk, Olivia keeps bouncing her leg up and down, and Eva's been twirling this one piece of hair on her finger for the last fifteen minutes. The room feels like it could blow any second, and Ponytail is just sitting up there in the front, reading his book and acting like he has no idea we're all on the verge of losing our minds. It's my third attempt at this geometry problem, and the numbers are all blurring into one another. I put my pencil to the paper. Then all of a sudden there's shouting in the back of the room and I can feel the energy shift, just like that, from silence and tension to full battle mode.

"What the fuck are you looking at, faggot?" It's the Compulsive Liar. He's out of his chair and throwing his insults in the general direction of Christopher, who's just sitting there looking stunned. Everyone else has turned around to watch, and no one looks surprised.

"Did you hear me, faggot?" Compulsive Liar says, all puffed up like a rooster, and Christopher shrinks in his seat. "I'm sorry?" he says, like he simply misheard. Who else but Christopher could be polite at a time like this?

"What's going on back there?" Ponytail says, but he sounds like he doesn't really want to know. I bet he'd rather just run out of the room and out of this place and drive home to his regular life, where he can read his book in peace. Compulsive Liar acts like he didn't even hear him, just keeps standing there staring at Christopher like he wants to kill him. I can't tell for sure, but I think Christopher is shaking. I can see his fists balled up. He's looking straight ahead, and I can only imagine what's going on in his head.

"Hey, faggot," Compulsive Liar says. "I asked you what you were looking at."

"I wasn't looking at anything," Christopher says, and the words barely make it through his clenched jaws. There's something on his face I haven't seen before, like a storm cloud building.

"You were looking at something, you piece of shit."

"Hey," Ponytail says, but he's not moving from his perch in the corner.

"I wasn't looking at anything," Christopher says again, and now Jason's getting out of his chair.

"What's the problem, Ryan?" Jason says, walking over from the other side of the room. He looks like somebody else all of a sudden, not like the pompous jerk who cares only about himself.

"This little faggot was looking at me," Compulsive Liar says, all chummy like he expects Jason to be on his side.

"Don't call me that," Christopher says, barely a whisper.

"What?" Jason and Compulsive Liar say in unison.

"I said don't call me that." Christopher's standing up now. "I'm sick of you calling me that." Jason steps back, surprised, like he doesn't recognize this kid standing in front of him who used to be Christopher. I don't recognize him either. I don't recognize anyone anymore.

"Faggot," Compulsive Liar says, and pushes Christopher in the chest. Ponytail's still at the front of the room, hiding behind his chair, calling for help on his walkie-talkie. Christopher falls back a little but catches himself and grabs the back of his chair, and then I blink, and just like that the chair's up in the air, and a sound like all the pain in the world is coming from somewhere inside Christopher's chest, and there's a look on his face like he's possessed, like this sweet homeschooled boy has been replaced by a young man full of rage, and the muscles in his neck tense, and the chair starts its slow-motion descent down onto Compulsive Liar's head, and I close my eyes, and Olivia screams, and I hear chairs being knocked over and the scrambling of feet away from the action.

When I open my eyes, the room is caught in freeze-frame, Jason in the middle with one hand on Compulsive Liar's chest and the other holding the chair in the air. Christopher lets go and hides behind him like he suddenly remembers who we all expect him to be.

"Get out of my way, Jason," Compulsive Liar growls.

"You are not going to fucking touch him," Jason says.

"You're defending this little faggot?"

"Didn't you hear him tell you not to call him that? I think he made himself very clear."

"I can't believe this," Compulsive Liar says, looking around for someone to agree with him. But Satan Worshipper went home yesterday, so now he's the last Scary Guy left, and he can't find anyone to meet his eye.

Jason sets Christopher's chair down as a counselor rushes in with two security guards. Ponytail's standing on a chair in the corner and pointing at Compulsive Liar, shouting, "That one started it," like a tattling child. Christopher's trying to pull away, but Jason's holding him by the shoulders now, looking him in the eyes and saying, "Calm down, man," and it feels like all of a sudden, just like that, we're not children anymore. Jason's a man and Christopher's a man, and they are standing there negotiating a man-size anger. This whole time, behind all his sweetness, Christopher has been holding a man-size pain, and behind all his childishness, Jason's been hiding a good man.

One of the security guards pulls Compulsive Liar's hands behind his back as he shouts curses at no one in particular. Ponytail climbs off the safety of his chair. Eva starts crying and throws her arms around Christopher, and we all relax and take a deep breath, and the air in our lungs is lighter than before. A feeling of relief spreads through the room, like somehow we needed this to happen.

GROUP

SHIRLEY: I heard we had some excitement during study hall yesterday.

CHRISTOPHER: It was awesome!

EVA: Oh my God, calm down. You're driving me crazy.

SHIRLEY: I have to say, Christopher, that's a pretty unusual reaction for you.

EVA: He's been like this since yesterday.

OLIVIA: He's probably still high off the adrenaline.

SHIRLEY: Can you try to explain how you're feeling?

KELLY: He's *been* explaining how he's feeling. He won't shut up about it.

CHRISTOPHER: I feel great, Shirley.

SHIRLEY: I'm glad to hear it.

CHRISTOPHER: Before yesterday I don't think I've ever yelled before. Can you believe that? Don't you think that's weird? That I've never yelled in my whole life?

SHIRLEY: This seems like huge progress for you. It sounds like you've never really given yourself permission to feel angry before.

CHRISTOPHER: Or stand up for myself either. I totally stood up for myself against that asshole.

EVA: You should have seen him.

SHIRLEY: I guess you guys don't even need me anymore.

CHRISTOPHER: Yeah, someone should be paying us.

SHIRLEY: I'm probably not supposed to openly support a patient losing his temper with another patient, but I'm proud of you, Christopher. I really am. But you're lucky Jason was there to stop you from inflicting physical damage.

CHRISTOPHER: I'm proud of me too.

EVA: Me too.

KELLY: Me three.

OLIVIA: Me four.

SHIRLEY: What about you, Jason?

JASON: Yeah, I'm proud of him too.

SHIRLEY: No, how do you feel about what happened yesterday? About your part in it?

JASON: I don't know. I didn't really have much of a part in it.

SHIRLEY: So modest. What I really mean to say is, how does it feel to not be such an asshole?

EVA: Whoa.

JASON: I'm still an asshole. Just because I did one semi-nice thing doesn't mean I'm not an asshole anymore. It doesn't make all the fucked-up shit I've done disappear. It doesn't un-hurt everyone I've hurt or make time go backward.

SHIRLEY: True. But even non-assholes do assholey stuff sometimes. It's called being human. Usually they can forgive themselves.

JASON: Yeah, well, most non-assholes aren't responsible for their kid sisters falling down the stairs and getting brain damage.

SHIRLEY: Dammit, Jason, listen to me. Look at my face. Are you listening?

JASON: Yes.

SHIRLEY: Listen carefully. Yes, you had a part in your sister's injury. There is no denying that. You were drunk, and your sister was an innocent victim of this deadly, fucked-up disease. And you have to live with that for the rest of your life. But listen to me carefully now. You did not *choose* to hurt her, Jason. Do you understand me?

JASON: Yeah, I guess.

SHIRLEY: You *did* choose to stand up for Christopher. You didn't have to do that. It wasn't an accident. It was you showing character. How do you feel about that? How does it feel to not be the piece of shit everyone's said you are your entire life? How does it feel to be a better man than your father raised you to be?

JASON: But I'm not.

SHIRLEY: Bullshit, Jason. I think you are. What if you could just consider that possibility? What if you could just forgive yourself?

CHRISTOPHER: I think you're a good person, Jason.

JASON: You think everybody's a good person.

CHRISTOPHER: But I know you are.

JASON: How do you know?

CHRISTOPHER: I just know.

JASON: I wish I believed you. I really do.

PERSONAL ESSAY

KELLY

Okay, so maybe I'm a little bitter. Maybe my childhood wasn't perfect. Maybe I have "unresolved anger" (they love that phrase around here). But the difference between me and everyone else in here is that it's not someone else's fault that I am the way I am. I can't be mad at my sick sisters or my parents who do everything they can to take care of them. What kind of person would I be then?

CHRISTOPHER

The thing about secrets is that God knows the truth even if you don't tell anyone. You can try to hide all you want, but there's no use. You can do all your schoolwork and act all normal at church, you can hide in your room and not bother anyone, but He's watching you and reading all your thoughts. So the only thing to do is confess, to admit your sins to God and ask His forgiveness. Be honest and trust God. That's what they've always told me. And I always believed them.

JASON

Then the whore started laughing. I will never forget the sound of her laugh. Like glass breaking. And then she called my dad in. "Dean," she said. "Dean, your fucking kid is a fag," ha, ha, ha, and he came in and looked at me like that's exactly what he had expected, like he accepted at that moment that I'd disappoint him forever. And he said, "Get the fuck out of here, Jason." He said, "Go watch TV for a while." And I left the bedroom. I closed the door behind me and turned the TV up loud.

EVA

Do you remember? Do you remember that first feeling of smoke filling your lungs? The spreading fog lifting you up. The gentle medicine healing everything that had been broken. And the magic bottle, the little white pills that made music when you shook them, the little white angels that made your body disappear. And the girl said, "Take me. Take my body and make me new."

OLIVIA

I come from a whole society of perfect people. But somehow, despite the work it takes to be perfect, everyone else at my school still seems to find the time for frivolous things like dating and parties. Somehow they are capable of having relationships with people besides their maids. It seems like I'm always scrambling to keep up, to maintain my position in the various hierarchies that fate signed me up for. I have no time for friends, let alone boyfriends. I barely have time to sleep. Everyone else makes it look so easy, like it's in their blood to be flawless and exceptional.

CHRISTOPHER

What I'm realizing is that sin is not as simple as I always thought. You can admit wrong actions and vow to change. You can say, "God, I've had a problem with drugs and now I'm going to stop." Then you get sober and He forgives you and you live happily ever after. But there's another kind of sin that goes deeper than action. What if your sin is not something you *do* but something you *are*? Something you can't change no matter how hard you try, no matter how much you pray, no matter how many times you ask God to change you? What if you don't change? What if you can't? What then?

KELLY

If I told you what kind of person I really am, you'd think I'm a monster. Because the truth is that sometimes I do hate my perfect family. Sometimes I wish my sisters had never been born and I'd gotten to keep all my parents' love. I fantasize about being even sicker than Shayla and Nicole, of having some condition even worse than theirs, like that would somehow punish everyone and get me what I want. How sick is that? To be competitive with your own sick sisters to see who can endure the most pain. And the winner is the one who does the best at threatening to die.

JASON

Have you ever tried not to cry? Like put every ounce of your being into it? Nothing I've ever done, no fights, nothing, has ever amounted to that kind of violence inside me. I remember sitting there, shaking, and I thought my fists were going to tear my hands apart. I remember a voice in my head, my father's voice, "Don't cry, you fucking pussy," and I've been hearing that same voice my entire life. I heard his grunts in the hotel bedroom, the naked woman's moans, and I have never in my life felt like less of a man.

EVA

And they made a circle around you, this new pack of misfits that did not judge. And you grew your shell like soft armor, until you were twice the size you were before. Even now that you were big, even now that no one could hurt you, you still kept your sadness like a secret, still grew thorns to keep it safe. Even now that you were not alone, you needed the medicine more than they did. Even though they thought they knew you, they did not know you needed the medicine more than you needed them.

OLIVIA

I have a secret theory that the hospital accidentally switched me at birth with my parents' real baby. Their real daughter is off in a suburb somewhere, astounding the whole town with her beauty and brilliance. But it should be me there instead, plain and nothing special. Mostly A's and B's, but not the top of the class. Maybe on the track team, but definitely not the star. Maybe I'd even be a little pudgy, and maybe I'd even be okay with that. Maybe I'd have a best friend I could talk to about everything, a group of girls to do things with after school and on the weekends. Sleepovers, walking aimlessly around the mall—isn't that what normal girls do? Maybe

I'd even have a boyfriend. He wouldn't have to be anything special either, not the most popular or smartest or richest. Just kind. And maybe a little funny. That would be nice. It would be nice to have at least kissed someone by now.

KELLY

I bet I could match up everybody with the right parents even if they weren't all sitting next to each other. As much as everyone tries to rebel with their clothes and hair and makeup, as much as we try to cover up every resemblance to the people who made us, it's really no use. I know I look exactly like my mom, and I'm okay with that. You should see pictures of her when she was in college— she could have won beauty pageants if she hadn't decided she was a feminist. And even though Christopher's about a quarter the size of his mother, they have the exact same baby face and nervous demeanor. The Pregnant Girl and her mom have the same birdlike appearance, with the same pointy nose and fluffy yellow hair. Eva gets her dark eyes from her father, the bad posture, the same tired and brooding attitude. The New Guy and his mom have the same kind blue eyes, except hers are lined with a couple decades' worth of worry.

But the scariest resemblance of all is between Jason and his father. It's like someone made a copy of Jason and just aged it thirty years. They're the same height and weight and build, with the same square jaw and broad shoulders. Something in Jason's face had softened over these few weeks, but the hardness came back as soon as his parents walked through those doors. It's like he was here at breakfast, but then I turned around and all of a sudden he was replaced by the old Jason, all wound up and pissed off and hating the world. His mom is like this little broken thing beside him, dressed up and painted in some kind of brave attempt to cover up the fact that she's barely there. Then there's Jason and his dad towering next to her, making her even smaller. There's something in his eyes that I haven't seen before, like something inside him is dead or hiding far away. It's no wonder he thinks it's impossible to get out from under his father's shadow—I'm sitting across the room and I swear I can feel how it's crushing him.

We've all heard this lecture before, the doctor's "What Is Addiction?" speech, the facts and science behind our self-destruction, the whats and hows and whys of our disease. The PowerPoint presentation shows how our brain synapses have been transformed, how we've turned into pleasure-seeking machines. Christopher's mother's face is twisted in a combination of confusion and anger, like she resents the doctor and all his difficult information. Jason's dad is sitting back in his folding chair with a smirk on his face like this is a waste of his time, Eva's dad is sad but attentive, and my parents are their own special brand of perky and earnest as they sit up straight in their chairs, eager for this doctor to tell them my secrets. This is the kind of thing that makes sense to them; this is a language they know. They know what to do with "disease." They know how to attach a doctor's medical descriptions to hope.

All the patients are in various states of discomfort about the fact that such a huge piece of them has been revealed, that this room full of teenage addicts and alcoholics we've been trying to impress for the last however many days has this sudden view into our lives, as if catching this glimpse of our parents allows them to see the most intimate parts of us. Some are probably afraid that their lies are going to be exposed, that everything they've ever said about their childhoods is going to be proven false—or even worse. We're afraid that even though we've told the truth, now everyone's going to take our parents' words over ours. The truth is, this is probably the first place most of us have ever had anyone believe us, where anyone has seen us as something other than a liar, a troublemaker, an all-around piece of shit. Our parents' presence threatens to take that away. It's like their being here negates everything we've worked so hard to become.

All of a sudden it hits me that I don't have much longer until I graduate from this place. Pretty soon I'm going to leave here and go back to the world that still thinks I'm someone I don't want to be anymore. I feel like running out of the room and locking myself in the bathroom and never coming out. At least I'd be safe in there. All they'd have to do is bring me my meals and I wouldn't bother anyone.

The room is packed with families, everyone with their eyes on the doctor in front of the room. Most people probably wouldn't even notice Olivia sitting over there in the corner, small and alone and practically invisible. Her parents didn't come. Her dad was too busy doing his important things, but her mom didn't even pretend to have an excuse. Olivia said she didn't care if they came or not, but of course no one believed her. Shirley said she would have liked to meet Olivia's mother so she could give her a little piece of her mind about prescription drug laws and responsible parenting. Whenever Shirley brings that up, Olivia gets really quiet, even quieter than usual. Sometimes I think she wants Shirley to tell someone what her mom did. I know I do. I want her mom to be punished somehow and I want her dad to know the truth; I want him to know it's not Olivia's fault. But maybe it's different when it's your own mom. Maybe no matter how awful she treats you, you still don't want to see her suffer.

So Olivia has to carry it all by herself and act like she's got everything under control. She's just sitting over there in the corner like an orphan. She's not even trying to impress everyone by taking notes like the last time we heard this lecture. She's just still and blank, like she's trying to disappear. I wish her mother was here so I could tell her exactly what I think. I want to tell her I believe Olivia. I want to tell her I know the truth. I want to show her all the hurt and anger she's made her daughter too afraid to feel.

The lecture's over, and practically all the parents' hands shoot into the air as soon the doctor announces he's open for questions. He calls on Christopher's mom first, and as she clears her throat, Christopher seems to shrink into himself. As she opens her mouth, the large rolls of flesh beneath her chin wiggle, and it's a mystery of science how someone so large could produce someone so small. The doctor asks her to introduce herself, and she says, "Oh, hello. I'm Mary-Ellen Morganson and this is my son, Christopher, and I just wanted to say that your theory's real nice for the real drug addicts in here, but my son just isn't like that. He's a good boy and a smart boy and he just made a few bad decisions and got led down the wrong path by someone he thought was his friend. So I'd like you to tell me, Doctor, if you have any suggestions how I as a mother can prevent him from going down the wrong path again, because I want to do everything I can to make sure he lives up to all his God-given potential. Thank you."

There are a few snickers in the room, most of them coming from other parents. Christopher's mom looks around like something hit her in the back of the head, and Christopher is hiding his face in his hands.

"With all due respect, Mrs. Morganson," the doctor says, "the most important thing for you to do for your son is acknowledge that he does indeed suffer from the disease of addiction. It will be very difficult for him to recover if he does not have the support of his family." My dad nods his head, and my mom reaches over and squeezes my hand, and something inside me breaks just a little.

"Of course I support him," she says. "How could you think I don't support him?" Christopher looks like he wants to crawl under his chair.

"Ma'am, I wasn't implying that at all," the doctor says. "Of course you love and support your son. I just want to emphasize how important it is that you acknowledge and respect his disease. He does not benefit from you thinking that he's somehow immune from it. This is an isolating disease, and telling your son he's different from everyone else can actually be harmful. It doesn't matter how smart and good a person is. Addiction and alcoholism are equal opportunity destroyers of lives."

"Yeah, I have something to say about that," Jason's dad announces from across the room, and Mrs. Morganson cowers at the sound of his big voice.

"Your name, sir?" the doctor says, and I swear he sounds a little defensive, like he's already prepared to not like him.

"Dean Ford, Dean Ford Construction, Bellevue, Washington. Jason here is my fuckup of a son. The thing is, Doctor, I just don't buy this disease idea. It sounds like an excuse to me, like some of that liberal propaganda people use to get out of taking responsibility for their actions." Christopher's mom says "Amen" quietly, and Eva's dad says to no one in particular, "Can you believe these people?"

"Mr. Ford, I understand your concerns," the doctor says, and even though I sort of hate him for never taking the time to learn my name, I have to give him some credit for handling our crazy parents. "I agree with you completely that our patients need to take responsibility for their actions. But we also can't expect to help them unless we get honest and make an effort to understand what makes them tick."

"Oh, I know what makes him tick, all right," Mr. Ford says, and I can see Jason's jaws working like they're going to grind themselves right out of his head. His hands are clenched into tight fists, and I'm glad I'm sitting all the way over here. It looks like either of them could explode any minute, and I don't want to be anywhere near them when that happens. Jason's mother seems to have shut down, like she's been trained to go into some kind of sleep mode when the hostility level gets to a certain level. It's like someone turned off a light switch inside her. I can't imagine what it must have been like to grow up in that house.

What's that expression? Tension so thick you could cut it with a knife? That's what it feels like in here. Even though everything seems calm and quiet on the surface, I wouldn't be surprised if a riot broke out and parents and children started tearing each other apart. "This is ridiculous," says a mother in the back, and several others grumble their agreement, and I guess I shouldn't be surprised that our parents aren't any better behaved than us.

The doctor raises his hand, and surprisingly, the room settles down enough for him to remind us that this is the time for questions related to the medical and practical aspects of addiction, and that we'll have two sessions of family group therapy to delve deeper into our feelings. That shuts everybody up, and there are a few moments of uncomfortable silence until my father raises his hand and says, "I for one would like to thank you, Doctor, for the work you do and this opportunity for healing that you've given my daughter." Someone goes, "Oh, God," and a couple people chuckle, and I can tell this is going to be a very long day.

CHRISTOPHER

This is hell. This is literally hell. If I had to choose the absolute worst way to spend eternity, it would be sitting in a folding chair next to my mother while she talks crazy in front of a bunch of strangers. I should probably start getting used to it since hell is where I'm probably going, with all the sinning I've done. If she gets her way, I'm coming with her to heaven, but I don't think she gets a whole lot of say in the matter. Maybe she'll get a replica of me in heaven to keep her company, and I'll get a replica of her in hell to embarrass me until the end of time.

All the kids from all the Groups, plus all their parents, are crammed together in the community meeting room for family group. Shirley is our fearless leader, with two ACs standing by like bodyguards. We're stuck sitting in these plastic chairs in this stuffy room for the next hour and a half, plus another session after lunch, like this is going to fix a whole lifetime's worth of crazy-making. Shirley told all the parents to each make a short statement about how their kids' drinking and drug use has affected their lives, and we're not allowed to say anything. We're expected to just sit here while they defame our character in front of our friends and a bunch of strangers.

Pregnant Girl's mom won't stop crying, and she has no one to comfort her. Pregnant Girl just sits there looking at her lap, at the small roundness just barely showing beneath her shirt. Everyone's trying to ignore the crying and act like it's no big deal to be listening to someone sobbing uncontrollably while hanging out with a bunch of kids and their parents at an adolescent treatment center. I don't know what kind of world they all live in, but I can tell you there is nothing natural about this.

All the parents keep talking, blah, blah, blah, and Shirley writes what they say on the whiteboard. Loss of trust, stealing, bad grades, getting arrested, all the pain we've caused them up there in big red letters while all the parents nod their heads and all the kids look either ashamed or angry. Eva is in the angry category, Kelly's ashamed, and Olivia's just looking out the window because her parents aren't here. Shirley said she'd still get something out of Family Day because she can relate to what other people are going through, but I don't think that's the point. It's not Olivia who needs Family Day. It's her stupid parents. They need to be here so someone can tell them what they did wrong and make them believe it. I don't know what kind of excuse they told Olivia, but I don't think she's surprised. And that's just sad, you know? To just expect your own parents not to show up for Family Day.

Jason, of course, is one of the angry ones. You can practically see the smoke coming out of his ears, and the daggers in his eyes when he looks at his dad. Before it was even his turn to speak, Jason's dad just blurted out, "My kid's responsible for his own sister's permanent brain damage. Top that." Like he was daring people to fight over whose kid is the bigger disappointment. Jason's mom gasped and put her hand to her mouth, acting like it was the first time she'd ever heard such a thing. She would fit right into my church with her pink dress, pink sweater, panty hose, and shoes. She's even wearing a pink headband. Everyone gets the message when they're a kid that girls like pink and boys like blue, but she's taken it to a whole new level, like being a girl is her religion and wearing pink is some kind of commandment. She's got her hands folded neatly in her lap, and her legs crossed at the ankles, and a pinched, pained expression on her face while her husband paints everyone a picture of her crappy son, Jason.

"Talk about a disappointment," Jason's dad says. "My kid told me he didn't want to try out for the football team. Tell me, what kind of kid doesn't want to be on the football team? Either a faggot or a fucking loser, that's who."

Jason flinches, and Shirley says, "Your language, Mr. Ford." He apologizes and continues with the same story probably everyone has—the grades slipping, the breaking curfew, the fighting and getting in trouble at school. Shirley says, "Raise your hand if you identify," and everyone except my mom raises their hand, and Jason's dad looks very pleased with himself. When everyone puts their hands down is when Mom decides to raise hers, and I would like to die right now, thank you very much.

"My son didn't do those things," she says. "Christopher's just been an angel his whole life." A few people chuckle, and Jason's dad goes, "Yeah, right, lady."

"Let's stay with Jason's family for right now, Mrs. Morganson," says Shirley, and I kind of want to hug her.

"He must have told you what he did to his sister," Mr. Ford says. Mrs. Ford starts fanning her face, and I can see the tears collecting in her eyes. Eva's dad hands Mrs. Ford a tissue. She thanks him and dabs at her eyes, but her husband keeps talking like he doesn't even know she's there. "Piece of shit got drunk and forgot he was watching her. Then she fell down the stairs headfirst, and now she's a retard and the doctors don't know if she'll ever talk again."

Parents mutter their condolences and pierce Jason with their dagger eyes, and Mr. Ford basks in the encouragement. "I should have just kicked him out of the goddamned house, pressed charges on his sorry ass, but his mother's soft, you know? Says he's her only son and we gotta give him another chance, send him here, send him to military school, maybe he can change. But I wanna know, when's the last chance? What if he fucks up at military school? He's not coming back home, I can tell you that much."

"That's definitely your choice, Mr. Ford," Shirley says.

"Damn right it is," he says.

"How do you feel about all of this, Mrs. Ford?" Shirley asks, and the woman practically jumps when she hears her name, like no one's ever bothered to ask her that before.

"Oh, she's too upset to say anything that makes sense," Mr. Ford says.

Shirley looks at him, hard. "If you don't mind, I'd like to hear what she has to say." Shirley looks at Mrs. Ford and tries to look encouraging.

"Well," Mrs. Ford says, wringing her hands. "I don't know what to say, really."

"Do you feel that the consequences for Jason's behavior have been appropriate?" Shirley asks.

"Oh, well, I don't know," she says, looking at her husband for some kind of instruction.

"Do you support the decision to send him to military school when he graduates from here?"

Mr. Ford turns and looks at her with a look that I could only describe as disgust, and I think about what happened between Jason and Kelly in the showers, and how it's pretty amazing really that Jason felt so bad about the way it turned out. It would be easy for him to be just like his father, to think of Kelly as something pathetic and unimportant, but Jason doesn't want to be like that. Everyone sees this big guy, and maybe they see someone like his dad, and maybe they assume he thinks and feels just like him. What they don't see is how hard he's trying to be someone else, someone bigger. They don't see how hard that is, don't recognize how much he's changed, and maybe the fact that he's still trying despite all that makes him bigger than all of us.

Mrs. Ford clears her throat and says in a voice like a little bird's, "I hope military school is good for him. I hope he learns things there. I hope he stops drinking."

"Jason," Shirley says. "How do you feel about that?"

"I hope the same things too," he says, and takes his

mother's hand in his. She looks up at him, and something changes in her face.

"Well, hell," Mr. Ford says. "Isn't that cute?" But I can tell he doesn't think there's anything cute about it, and all of a sudden Eva's dad goes, "For Pete's sake, shut the hell up." Everyone pretty much stops breathing, like we're all expecting Mr. Ford to go ballistic and start beating everybody up.

"Excuse me?" Mr. Ford says, and Mrs. Ford shrinks into a little pink ball, and Jason straightens up like he's about to go to war, and Eva's got this look on her face like, *What the hell happened while I was busy not paying attention?* Even though her dad's balding and his clothes look wrinkled, there's something cool about him, like he's not scared of Jason's dad at all.

"You think you're some kind of tough guy?" he says, and everybody's looking at one another like they can't believe how dumb he is. "You think it's tough to be a fifty-year-old bully and belittle your wife in public and humiliate your son? You think that's what we're supposed to be doing here?"

"I'd watch your mouth if I were you, little man," Mr. Ford says. Mrs. Ford has her hands in front of her face, like she believes everything will go away if she just doesn't look at it.

"Little man?" Eva's dad says. "For your information I have two PhDs and I'm head of the sociology department at the University of Washington. Guys like you empty out my wastebasket."

"Oh my God, Dad. Stop!" Eva says, and women start grabbing their purses like they're getting ready to flee.

"Everyone, calm down!" Shirley says. And, amazingly, they do. She's the only person I ever met who could get a room to settle down like this. Everyone sits up straight and looks right at her, and for a second everyone, the kids and the parents, are all the same size.

"I know we're all a little tense," she says. "You are all dealing with years of built-up feelings. You're scared and you are angry, justifiably so. No one said this was going to be easy. But as hard as this is, and as much as I sympathize with each and every one of you, there will be no tolerance for disrespect in this room. Do you understand me?" Parents and kids both nod their heads. Mrs. Ford takes her hands away from her face. My mom says a little prayer under her breath.

"Mr. Jacoby? Is that your name?" Shirley says to Eva's dad.

"*Dr.* Jacoby. Yes," he says, and Eva rolls her eyes.

"Would you care to share how you feel about Eva's drug use?"

"Yes, I would, thank you," he says. Eva could be the poster girl for angry teenagers right now. She's slouching down, with her arms crossed over her chest and a big old scowl on her face. "Well, I'm disappointed," he says. "That's the main thing.

Her mother and I didn't raise her to be some dropout. She's smart. She has a future. This is just childish, really. I mean, I understand it's fun to smoke a joint once in a while, but at a certain point you have to get serious and start thinking about what's important, like getting into a good college. She's sixteen already. She should have already figured out where she wants to apply for early decision."

"Eva, how do you feel about what your father just said?" Shirley asks.

"Yeah, I know all that," she says. "It's not like I want to be a loser either. I have ambitions. I have dreams. Maybe he would know that if he was paying any attention."

"Mr. Jacoby—I'm sorry, *Dr.* Jacoby—are you hearing what Eva's saying?"

"Yes, but that doesn't change the fact that she's gotten so addicted to prescription drugs that she has to be here and taking detox medications. Her mother and I didn't raise her like this."

"Well, maybe it wouldn't have gotten this bad if you would have noticed something was wrong a long time ago," Eva says. "It's not like I ever wanted to be a drug addict. It's not like I wanted to end up in rehab at age sixteen addicted to fucking pain pills. Who would want that? I'm not fucking stupid."

"Watch your mouth, young lady," says her dad.

"Dr. Jacoby," Shirley says. "Do you think you were paying attention?"

"I can't watch her every second. I have a lot of work to do."

"And a lot of drinking to do," Eva says under her breath, but you can tell she wanted everyone to hear, and you can tell that they did, because the room gets very quiet. Her dad looks at her with his eyes wide, almost like he's never seen her before and now, all of a sudden, there she is right in front of him and he doesn't know what to do about it.

"See, Dad," Eva says. "Even if you weren't paying attention, I was." And just like that, Eva's no longer the tough girl she tries to be all the time. All of a sudden she's crying like nothing can ever make her stop, and her body is shaking with big sobs, one after another after another. I want to do something. The New Guy looks like he wants to run over there and hug her. But that's not our job right now. Neither of us is the one who's supposed to be doing that.

"Eva," her father says softly. "Oh, Eva, I'm sorry." He puts his arm awkwardly around her, and you can tell he hasn't done that in a very long time.

"Dr. Jacoby," Shirley says more gently than I've ever heard her. "I can't help but notice that you've referred to your deceased wife twice in the last few minutes."

He looks up but says nothing.

"Dr. Jacoby," Shirley says, "do you think you have a drinking problem?"

Eva looks at him with something that looks like hope.

"It's been hard," he says.

"What's been hard?" says Shirley.

"Since my wife died."

"Yes."

"Dad?" Eva says. He looks at her, and maybe it's that simple, really. Maybe that's all she ever wanted. "It's been hard on me, too." That's when he starts crying, and let me tell you, I don't think there's anything sadder than watching a grown man cry.

"I just can't believe she's gone," he says, weeping.

"I know. Me neither," Eva says. "But I'm still here."

Then they hug, and probably half the people here have tears in their eyes, and I know I'm supposed to be happy for them. Eva's my friend and she deserves to have a father who cares about her and supports her. She deserves to go home after this place and share a home with someone who will at least try to understand who she is and maybe take some responsibility for it. And I am happy for her. I really am. But I can't help but hate her too. And I know how bad that is, and I know I'm going to hell for feeling that way. But I cannot take the high road this time. I'm tired of always taking the high road. Because the truth is I'm jealous of Eva and everyone in here. I'm even jealous of Jason, because at least he gets to go to military school and get away from his crazy family until he turns eighteen and gets set free. I'm jealous and I'm angry that I have none of what they have. After this place I'm going to go right back where I started, trapped inside that house to wait on my giant crazy mother all day long, back to that life where I'm the homeschooled church kid and nothing else. Even if I want to change, I can't. I'm going back to a world that only wants me if I stay exactly the same. I should just be honest and give up right now. Even though I want to change, even though I want it more than I've ever wanted anything, the truth is, I need help and I can't do it alone and my mother is never going to change the way I need her to.

DRUG & ALCOHOL HISTORY QUESTIONNAIRE

QUESTION #5:

What are your plans for staying sober?

stop hanging out with old friends

keep busy   change schools

do volunteer work

develop a sober support network

find a hobby   start painting

write in a journal

continue with outpatient treatment

go to recovery meetings

see a therapist

follow my relapse prevention plan

avoid triggering places and people

avoid situations and places where drugs and alcohol will be available

be honest about my feelings

exercise   take responsibility for my actions

eat healthy

get plenty of sleep   make sober friends

meditate   spend more time with my family

pray   ask for help

laugh   only hang out with people

who support my recovery

forgive the people who have hurt me

forgive myself

get a job

set goals

focus on going to college

think about the person I want to be and the life I'd like to have

remind myself how bad it was

change everything

KELLY

Olivia isn't the only one

not eating this morning. Everyone seems to be poking at their food, staring off into space, not talking. I guess we're all a little traumatized by Family Day. No one wants to talk about it. No one's looking each other in the eye. Even Eva and the New Guy are barely acknowledging each other's existence. It's like we all got drunk last night and woke up naked and in bed together and don't want to acknowledge what must have happened. Talking about it just makes it real.

The five of us are some of the people who have been here the longest. Almost everyone who was here on my first day is gone, and a new crop has taken their place. What a strange thing this is—I'm going to be forty years old some day and telling people I went to rehab when I was seventeen. It is a permanent chapter in my story, something I cannot undo, a page I cannot rip out. There is no pretending that things will ever be normal, that I will ever be the daughter my perfect parents should have had. Even if I heal, even if I recover, this will always be my past and it will always be a part of me.

I think before I ever became an alcoholic, before I even tasted alcohol or tried drugs, I was already programmed to be this way. Before there was cocaine or vodka or sex or any of that, there was fantasy. There was escape. That was my first addiction. I remember being a little kid and imagining everything different, myself different. How did I get the idea in my head at age eight that everything was better somewhere else? Why would a child have a hole inside that can't get full no matter what she does? The real world could never make me happy, so I retreated to the world inside my head. And as I grew, as the real world proved itself more and more painful, the fantasy world expanded.

I look around at the newer kids here and realize that they look like a different species from us. They look so tired, so angry, and even the black kid looks pale. There's something missing in their eyes. It may sound like a cliché, but I see it—something is definitely dead inside. And how does that make any kind of sense? We're fucking children. This is the most alive we should ever be. Kids with cancer, with AIDS, with terminal diseases—my sisters—they have an excuse. But not us. We did this to ourselves.

The boy over there has the shakes. He arrived late last night. He can barely keep a spoon in his hand. He's only fifteen.

The new girl with the neck tattoo looks like a ghost because she's been puking all morning.

The guy in the corner is fast asleep and snoring because he'd been up for four days before coming here.

I remember that feeling. The first day. The second day. When the world is as small as the thin layer of air touching your skin. When all that exists is your almost-dead body and the pain inside your head. There is no tomorrow or a few days from now. There is no college or love or children or career. There is only now and the burning synapses in your head, the ache in your chest, the molten lava in your stomach. The emptiness. The need. The desperation. And the fear.

The fear.

That this pain is all you'll feel for the rest of your life.

The Pregnant Girl is leaving today. She just started crying uncontrollably and her Group is trying to comfort her. She keeps saying, "What am I going to do? What am I going to do?" over and over again. And no one has an answer for her.

No one could possibly know what a pregnant sixteen-year-old girl should do. All her friends can do is hold her hand and be with her until her mom comes to take her away, to take her back to the life that got her in here.

The new kids look at her like she's a nuisance. They want her to shut up. There is only enough room in the world for them right now, each of them in their little pocket of space. Their world is so small that their only option is to be selfish.

The first week is the hardest. Then little by little the world opens up, and you realize there are all these people around you with their own needs that have nothing to do with you. Then you forget, and everything's about you again. And maybe that cycle continues for the rest of your life. Maybe the world keeps expanding and contracting. Maybe you know you're well when it finally stays the same size.

Olivia looks sicker than usual this morning. Family Day must have been hard on her. She hasn't even bothered to get a plate of food to pretend to eat.

"Hey, Olivia," I say. "You okay?"

She nods her head weakly, not even looking up.

"You don't look okay," says Eva.

Olivia makes an attempt at a smile. "I just have a headache."

I wonder what her life is going to be like after this. How can she look her mother in the eye? How could they possibly live in the same house pretending nothing happened? I don't think I could keep a secret like that. My anger wouldn't let me. But it's like Olivia has shoved hers down so deep she doesn't even know where to find it. She's programmed herself so thoroughly that messy feelings like anger don't fit anywhere. But it must be somewhere in there, simmering, gaining strength. This is the kind of thing you see on TV—the quiet person who just loses it one day. It is the thing of police dramas. Just like that, the character cracks and wreaks havoc, and a police psychologist has a monologue about how the trauma of their past created a hibernating monster. Then the monster wakes up and nothing is ever the same again.

But Olivia won't turn into a monster. She won't lose her mind one day and go on a killing spree and end up on a *Law & Order* episode. What I'm afraid of is that she'll destroy herself, turn her pain inward until it kills her. And the whole time everything will look perfect on the outside. No one will know she's dying until she's dead.

"Really, Olivia," Christopher says. "You don't look good."

"I think we should get the nurse," says the New Guy.

Olivia puts her hand on her forehead and closes her eyes.

"What's wrong?" I ask her.

"My eyes," she says.

"What's wrong with your eyes?"

"Everything's glowing."

Eva stands up. "Okay. We're going to the nurse *now*."

We all stand up. Jason notices from his table across the dining room and stands up too. Olivia rises, and we all circle around her, grabbing at her, anticipating her fall.

"Stop hovering," she says with a little laugh, and that makes me smile. It's a sad joke, and we all know it. I doubt her parents have ever shown her this kind of concern.

We start walking toward the door. Everyone's looking at us. The AC in charge says, "Hey, where you guys going?" He's a new guy with a big scar across his cheek and dressed in denim from head to toe. It seems like we have a new AC almost every day. I guess it takes a special person to do this kind of job. I guess most of them figure out quickly that they aren't that person.

"She's going to the nurse," Jason says, taking charge. I think he'll do well in military school. His arm touches mine, and I don't flinch. I know I should hate him, but I don't.

We're almost to the door when Olivia goes limp and falls to the ground.

Her body starts jerking. Her legs kick. I feel her feet kicking my legs.

"Oh, God," someone says.

Her eyes are closed. Her skin is suddenly porcelain. She

is hard and fragile and she is going to crack. There is no life inside.

"Oh, God."

"Someone protect her head!" Jason yells, and Eva crouches down and collects her, holds her in her lap. "Olivia," she says. "Olivia, *please*."

Her lips are turning blue and the floor is a puddle around her. She has wet herself. Olivia, you have finally lost control.

"Someone get the nurse!" Jason yells, and Christopher goes running. The new AC runs over but seems to know Jason's in charge now. Olivia keeps shaking, and there is a thin line of blood trailing down her chin.

"Oh, God," someone says again.

God. Why would you do this to her? She doesn't deserve this. All she's ever done is try to be good.

Olivia's body goes limp. Everything is still. No one moves or makes a sound.

"Olivia," Jason says.

She doesn't move. I can't tell if she is breathing.

"Olivia."

Nothing.

"Oh, God!" I scream. It has been me saying it this whole time. Oh God oh God oh God oh God. Please, God. *Please.*

CHRISTOPHER

Come here," Eva says,
and pulls my arm.

"Ouch," I tell her, even though it didn't really hurt, but
she can't just go around pulling on people's arms like that. It's
after community meeting and everybody's outside smoking
as usual. They're still talking about Olivia's seizure, and I just
can't take it anymore. I've been staying as far away from anyone
not in my Group as I can, because it just makes me mad to
hear them talk. It's like they have no right to say anything,
because when did they ever talk to her? When were they ever
nice to Olivia? They have no right to start pretending they're
best friends now.

Eva's still pulling on my arm and it's actually starting to

hurt, so I say, "What do you want, Eva?" and she stops pulling and looks at me and says, "Christopher, what happened to you?" and I'm like, "What do you mean, what happened to me?" So she says, "You've changed," and I say, "Of course I've changed. I'm three weeks sober and my friend is in the hospital," and she says, "It's more than that." I don't really have anything to say to that, so I just stand there looking at her, trying to ignore the hot, tight feeling in my stomach and chest that keeps coming up all the time, that's been pretty much permanent since yesterday.

"You're, like, really grumpy," she says, so I say, "I, like, totally have a right to be grumpy." Then she says, "But you're, like, never grumpy," and I'm getting really tired of this conversation and every other single conversation I've been having lately. "What's your point?" I ask her, and she just says, "Come with me," and starts walking toward the stairs that go upstairs, even though everyone's still on the smokers' patio and we're not allowed to leave the area. "Where are you going?" I say, and she doesn't say anything, doesn't even turn around. I look behind me, and the ACs are busy watching everyone on the patio, and everyone on the patio is busy watching each other, so nobody notices Eva walking into forbidden territory.

"Eva, you're breaking the rules," I say, but I follow her up the stairs anyway.

"So tell on me," she says.

"We're going to get caught," I say.

"So turn around," she says, but I don't. I keep following her, but I don't know why. I'm supposed to be the good kid, right? I'm supposed to follow the rules and not get in trouble and be a perfect little angel all the time, but maybe I'm getting tired of that. Maybe I want to do something else for a change. Look where being the good kid got Olivia. In a hospital, probably with tubes coming out of her everywhere.

Eva stops at the top of the stairs, and I run into her. "Hey," I say, and she goes "Shhh" with her finger in front of her mouth like I'm in trouble for talking in church. "Where are we going?" I whisper. "Just be quiet," she says, then pokes her head into the hall and looks around. She motions to say the coast is clear, and I notice a new feeling in my chest, something much nicer than what's been there lately, something lighter, electric, almost like the feeling I used to get from meth or coke. She whispers, "Channel your inner ninja, Christopher," and before I have a chance to ask her what she's talking about, she runs across the hall to the big fire door by the bathrooms, the one with the big sign with red letters that says DO NOT ENTER, and I run after her without thinking, and it's like one of those war movies where the soldiers jump out of their hiding spot and start running exposed, trying to dodge enemy bullets as they head toward safety. Except this is not a war zone, it's just a glorified clinic in a suburb of Seattle, and I don't know what I'm running from and I don't know where I'm going.

We're at the door and her hand's on the metal handle, and she's got a look in her eye like anything is possible. "What are you doing?" I ask her.

"What does it look like I'm doing?" she says.

"You can't get out this way."

"How do you know?"

"There's no way out."

"Of course there is," she says. "There's always a way out. They just tell us we're trapped here, and we don't question it. But I bet you a million dollars we can just walk right out and no one will notice."

"You're crazy."

"I dare you, Christopher," she says. "I dare you to break the rules, just this once."

The feeling in my chest gets stronger. The electricity spreads into my shoulders and down my arms until I can feel it tingling in my fingers. "But I don't want to leave," I say, and I mean it, but something about it feels like lying, like we're talking about something entirely different from what we're talking about.

"Don't worry, Christopher," she says. She grabs my hand, and the warmth in hers mixes with the electricity in mine.

"But I want this, Eva," I say. "I want to stay sober."

"I do too," she says. "We're not running away. We're going to come right back."

"What are you talking about?"

"We're just taking a little vacation." She smiles and looks me in the eye. "Don't you need a vacation, Christopher? You've been serious your entire life."

I hear the door open downstairs, then the voices of everyone coming back in from the patio. A surge of electricity shoots through me, and I realize right then that Eva's right. I do need a vacation. I need to do something, anything, that's different from everything I've ever done before.

Without saying anything we push together and the door opens just like any other door. No alarms go off, the sky doesn't fall, we're not sent straight to hell for breaking the rules. I breathe in the fresh, cool pine-scented air. I feel my heart beating fast inside my chest. Eva says, "Go," and we start running.

We run and run and I don't know how long we run. I just know that the air feels good against my face and down my nose and in my lungs. Everything in my body stings like little pinpricks, but I keep running. Eva's breathing sounds painful, but she's got a look on her face like pure bliss, and I feel like laughing, this feels so good.

"Scream," she yells at me.

"What?" I yell back.

"Just start screaming." And then she opens her mouth wide and a great big "Aaah" comes out, so I do it too. I open my mouth and just push.

We're running down the street screaming like a couple of crazy people, the trees and quiet houses whipping around us. Cars drive by, and I don't care what they think. All I care about is the stinging in my lungs, the burning in my legs, the cold tears in my eyes, my voice loud and raw and ugly. Eva slows down and turns, her eyes wild. "Fuck," she says, and hunches over and tries to catch her breath. "Fuck," she says again.

"Are you okay?"

"Fuck yes," she says. "I'm better than okay." She manages to steady her breathing a little. "Damn, I need to get into shape."

There's a little park up the road, so I start running toward it. "No more running!" Eva yells, and hobbles behind me. I want to keep moving. I never want to be still again.

"Just a little farther," I say.

"Listen to you." She laughs between wheezes. "You're such a rebel."

I reach the park and find a swing and start swinging. I don't know when the last time was that I was on a swing. It feels like I haven't been outside in forever. Eva gets on the one next to mine and we don't say anything for a while, just keep swinging, up and down and up and down, flying and falling at the same time.

"How are you feeling?" she says after a while.

"Great," I tell her, and I don't remember ever feeling this good without drugs. Even then there was always something not quite right, like this anxiety under every good feeling, a yearning for something else, a tight ache that would keep me on edge.

"See," she says. "And you didn't even want to come."

"Eva, you're crazy," I tell her, and I mean it in the nicest way possible.

"Thanks," she says. "You are too."

We just swing for a while, and the chains make a squeaking sound, like metal breathing, and I start thinking about Todd, about how in all those months of him climbing into my room at night, we never once did anything like this. We never just sat together like this, comfortable, not using each other for something. And all the other kids at church that I've known for as long as I can remember, we've never even known each other at all.

"Thank you," I say to Eva, and she doesn't have to ask what for. She just smiles and nods and keeps swinging.

"You know what?" she says.

"What?"

"I think it's going to be okay."

"What is?"

"I don't know. Just . . . *it.*"

"Oh," I say, and then I feel a little pinch of sadness, because maybe I'm not so sure about that anymore, that things are going to be okay. Because in these last three weeks the world's gotten bigger than it's ever been in my whole life, and I realize I don't understand any of it. I've always had faith, that blind sureness I was taught by my mother and my church, but I'm starting to think I need more than that to get through this.

"Eva, can I tell you something?" I say.

"Is it that I'm beautiful?"

That makes me smile. The Eva I met three weeks ago would never have said something like that.

"Yes, that's one of the things I wanted to tell you," I say, and she smiles and closes her eyes and points her face to the sky, and she is beautiful, she really is.

"You know the guy Todd I've talked about?" I say. "The one I did all the meth with?"

"Uh-huh."

"He didn't make me pay." I don't know why I'm telling her this. I didn't think I'd ever tell anyone. We were just sitting here swinging, and out of nowhere this thing was in my mouth, all sharp and hard and cold. I was thinking about faith and how it's not everything anymore, and all of a sudden there was this new thing in its place, this truth, and my mouth had to open to let it out.

Eva looks at me with something new in her eyes, something familiar, something I think I used to have. It's the stillness that comes from trusting that everything's going to turn out just the way it needs to. I don't know where or how she got it, or how long it's going to last, but it looks beautiful on her.

"I did other things," I tell her. "He made me do other things."

She doesn't say anything, just looks at me with that look in her eyes that says I can tell her anything and she'll still be there, she won't run away.

"At first I didn't want to. He was mean about it. Violent. He said he'd kill me if I told anyone. But after a while he didn't have to force me. I just did it. After a while I started wanting to."

She reaches out her hand and wraps her fingers around mine. Our swings are out of sync for a few moments, but slowly they catch up until we're swinging in time. She squeezes my hand, and I know I don't have to tell her that I enjoyed it, but I do anyway. I tell her that even though he was cruel and dumb, even though I was scared and ashamed, my body had a mind of its own. I tell her how I learned to close my eyes and pretend it wasn't him, how I could pretend he was handsome and kind and gentle, how I could pretend he loved me and he didn't think what we were doing was disgusting, that I was disgusting for wanting it. The thing is, you don't get many choices when you're stuck in a secret. The world gets so small, you learn to be grateful for whatever you can get.

"Did you love him?" Eva says.

"I don't know," I say. "I hope not. I hope love feels different from that."

We hold hands for a long time, swinging limply, our feet scraping the gravel beneath us. It's like we're on the cover of some morbid Hallmark card, two kids waiting in a park on the edge of a funeral. The scene is a muddy pastel, with tiny versions of ourselves. Eva is wearing a frilly dress and pigtails, and I'm in an oversize tuxedo and top hat. You can tell from the picture it's going to rain soon, even if you can't feel the moisture in the air, even if you can't smell it.

It's cold and we're not wearing coats, and the sweat from our running absorbs into our clothes and our bones. Eva's hand seems like the only warm thing I have ever touched, and I love her at this moment more than I have ever loved anyone.

"Are you ready to go back?" she says.

"Almost," I tell her. I take a deep breath, feel the cold air in my lungs, taste the pine from nearby trees, taste the smoke from a distant chimney. I feel the sharp wetness of drizzle on my face. I breathe in, close my eyes, feel the swirling of life and faith and truth inside me. I breathe out, and they are all still there.

"Okay," I say. "I'm ready."

KELLY

In the next few days

we'll all be gone. Jason graduates tomorrow. Then he's off to military school. It's me the next day, then Christopher and Eva. Olivia was supposed to go home after that, but who knows what's going to happen now.

After we're all gone, Shirley will have a brand-new Group and will probably never think about us again. I wonder how many kids filter through here in a year, how many broken lives they attempt to put back together. I wonder how often they succeed. I've heard the statistic that only 10 percent of us stay sober for a year after graduating. What about the other 90 percent? Were the rest of us just a waste of time? Are we going to spend the rest of our short lives getting higher and higher until we can't get high anymore? What then?

Or maybe some of us just aren't done yet. Maybe we'll choose recovery eventually, but just not yet. Maybe this was just practice and we collected everything we learned here, filed it away to use later when we decide we really need it. Later, because we're so young and we have years' worth of partying left in us. Later, because we still have time before we hit rock bottom.

But Olivia—I don't think she has another bottom left. How can there be any lower for her to go?

The rest of us, I don't know. Even though we're only sixteen or seventeen, maybe this is our last chance. Or maybe it's not. The scary thing is that there's no way of knowing. I want to be one of the 10 percent who make it, but how many of us say that, and how many of us end up drunk a few days later? Maybe I'll get out in the real world and forget everything I learned in here. Maybe the voice will come back, the one that tells me I have everything under control, that I shouldn't worry, that it's okay to relax and have a drink even though everything is falling apart, because a drink is the only thing that can fix it. And maybe that voice will win, and it'll put those drinks in my hand and it'll put that coke in my nose, and it'll tell me it's okay to drive. But this time it won't be the neighbor's porch and rosebushes that suffer. This time it will be someone's sister or friend or father or daughter, and I will have traded their life for the chance to get high.

For now it is activity hour and my last time on this decrepit playground. I'm walking alone on the edge of the baseball field while everyone else plays basketball or four square. Besides Jason, everyone here is a stranger. Olivia's in the hospital, and Eva and Christopher are stuck back at the facility because they're on probation for their little runaway performance. So it's just me and Jason, the last of the old guard, waiting to be let back into the real world.

I run my hand across the chain-link fence and feel it cold against my fingers. Part of me wants to grab on and squeeze until the metal turns sharp and prints into my skin, until pressure makes it a weapon. I feel like pressing up against it and feeling it cut into my face, brand my skin with its crisscross pattern. I walk and walk and the mud sticks to my shoes, but I don't care. I'm not trying to impress anyone. I may never try to impress anyone again.

I hear something *squish, squish, squish* behind me, something large and fast approaching quickly. I turn around slowly, expecting to see a dog or maybe an AC who decided I've walked far enough. Instead it's Jason, panting slightly, his face red and a little sweaty. This is the closest I've been to him in more than a week. I flinch when he says "Hi."

"Sorry," he says. "I didn't mean to scare you."

"Don't worry about it."

"Is it okay that I'm talking to you?" he says. "I mean, I'll go away if you want me to."

"What do you think?" I say. "Should I want you to go away?"

"Probably," he says, then it's like a sad cloud passes over his face, and part of me feels bad, like it's somehow my fault he's been so depressed lately. I know I shouldn't feel that way. I know I have every right to be mad at him. But I've been thinking a lot lately, about all sorts of things, but mostly about how we're all a lot more complicated than any of us probably think we are.

"Your parents seem really nice," he says.

"Yeah, they are," I say. "If there was an award for World's Nicest Parents, they'd definitely be contenders."

"How was Family Day for you?"

"It was okay. You?"

"Couldn't you tell?" he says. "Major breakthroughs all day long. All of my family problems are officially fixed."

"Yeah, right," I say. It's good he has a sense of humor about it. I don't know if I could if I were him.

"You're really lucky, you know?" he says.

"Yeah, I know." After seeing everybody's parents on Family Day, fuck yes, I know I'm lucky.

We walk for a while not saying anything. Everyone else is on the other side of the field, bouncing balls off concrete. We're in a residential neighborhood in the middle of a workday, so everything is eerily quiet. It's just the two of us and the squishing of our muddy footsteps, and even though I know I'm supposed to hate him, I feel strangely comfortable. Something about the gray sky and the gray fence and the fact that this is one of the last times we'll ever speak, something about all that makes this moment weirdly sentimental.

"I need to tell you something," Jason says, and I'm neither surprised nor scared. If there was ever an appropriate time to tell each other something, it would be right now.

He stops walking. I look at him and realize he wants me to stop walking too. This is going to be the kind of conversation that requires standing perfectly still. "Kelly," he says, and I look him in the eye. Something has definitely changed.

"I've been thinking a lot about what I wanted to say to you," he begins. "Nothing I say will ever be enough. Maybe someone else could do it better, someone smarter who knows more words. But all I can do is do my best, right?"

I nod, because I can feel that he wants some kind of

encouragement. This should probably make me happy, this new humility of his, this thoughtful new Jason. But I don't know if I should trust him. Maybe this is just another one of his jokes.

"I'm not going to try to make excuses for what I did to you, because it's inexcusable," he says. I feel a dull pain inside my chest at this reminder of what happened, a remnant of the fear I felt in that tiny shower stall. But another feeling comes with it, something the opposite of scary, something that feels strong and sturdy and not scared of anything.

"I have a lot of shit to figure out," Jason says. "A lot of really fucked-up shit I thought I understood. I could try to explain to you how I grew up with bad examples and that's why I turned out all fucked up. But the truth is everyone has to take responsibility for their actions eventually, and I need to take responsibility for mine."

I nod again because I can't say anything. I'm afraid that if I open my mouth, more than words will come out—all my tears and sobs and snot, all my gratitude and pain, all my crazy wishing that he was speaking for every boy and every man who's ever touched me.

"I think that's what finally makes us adults, you know?" he says. "It's when we stop blaming our parents for everything and realize we're making our own choices."

"Yeah," I say, and my voice breaks a little.

"What I'm basically trying to say, Kelly—" He pauses, and I look up, and I realize he was waiting to continue until he could look me in the eye. "What I'm trying to say is you didn't deserve that. You didn't deserve how I treated you. You don't deserve to be treated like that by anyone."

I close my eyes. I feel my feet planted solidly in the mud beneath me. Something inside my chest feels a little cleaner, a little lighter, like someone went in there and scrubbed out all the crap that's been building up for years. Maybe it's because of Jason, or maybe it's just the cold air. Maybe it's neither of those things. Maybe it's just me.

"I know," I tell him, and maybe I actually believe it.

GROUP

SHIRLEY: There's not much in the way of news, I'm afraid. Olivia's father flew out as soon as we called him, and he's been by her side at the hospital. He's keeping me posted, but there isn't a whole lot to report. They're still doing tests. But he wanted me to thank you all for being such good friends to Olivia.

EVA: Did he turn his fucking bitch wife in to the police yet?

CHRISTOPHER: Yeah.

SHIRLEY: I know you're going to hate me for this, but that kind of information needs to stay confidential right now.

If Olivia wants to tell you about it, that's her choice. But it is not my place to talk about it with you.

EVA: That's bullshit.

SHIRLEY: Would you want me telling anybody private stuff about you?

EVA: But we're not just anybody.

SHIRLEY: I know, and I'm sure Olivia would want to talk to you about it, but she's the one who needs to make that decision, not me. It would be unethical for me to make that decision for her.

KELLY: God, this sucks.

SHIRLEY: Yes, it does. But I can assure you she's going to get the help she needs now, and it's more help than we could offer her here.

KELLY: But why couldn't we help her? Why weren't we enough?

SHIRLEY: We're not a treatment center for eating disorders, Kelly. She is very sick and needs very specialized help.

KELLY: But it's not like you don't know anything about

eating disorders. You studied it in school, right? The doctor knows things. You should have done something. Shirley, why didn't you do anything?

JASON: Kelly, calm down.

KELLY: No. Fuck you. This is bullshit. We were supposed to watch out for her. We were supposed to make sure she was eating. Me, I was. I was supposed to be paying attention.

CHRISTOPHER: It's not your fault.

KELLY: I was supposed to be watching her. That was my job. Shirley said it was my job, remember? She cut herself. Did you know that? I saw the scars. I didn't tell anyone. I didn't tell. We could have helped her.

SHIRLEY: Kelly, look at me.

KELLY: No.

SHIRLEY: Kelly, goddammit, look at me right now.

KELLY: It's all my fault.

SHIRLEY: No, it's not. Listen to me. You were a good friend to her. You all were. You are the best friends she's ever had.

KELLY: But we could have done more.

SHIRLEY: Maybe. Sure. You could have held her down and shoved food into her mouth. But do you really want that job? Do you really think that's what she needed from you?

KELLY: I don't know.

SHIRLEY: You did the best thing you could have possibly done for her. You were her friend. You helped her more than you'll ever know.

KELLY: I don't believe you.

SHIRLEY: I have regrets too, you know.

CHRISTOPHER: You do?

SHIRLEY: I know this will come as a total shock to you, but I'm not perfect either. I know, I know, it's unbelievable.

CHRISTOPHER: I never thought you were perfect, Shirley.

SHIRLEY: Thank you, Christopher. Seriously, though. Olivia needed more than we could ever give her here. I should have seen that. And there are things I should not have let her keep secret.

EVA: Yeah. Her fucking mom. I'm going to kill her.

SHIRLEY: Is that a threat? You know I have to report that.

EVA: Very funny.

SHIRLEY: You know, this is our last Group with everyone together.

JASON: We know.

EVA: We're trying not to think about it.

SHIRLEY: I want you to know how proud I am.
Of all of you.

CHRISTOPHER: Are we your favorite Group ever?

SHIRLEY: I'm afraid that information is classified.

CHRISTOPHER

I swear this lady is the sober, grown-up version of Eva. She's big and beautiful and she's got the same black hair and punky clothes and sarcastic sense of humor. The main difference is she smiles a lot more and she's always giving everybody hugs, which I just cannot see Eva doing. I'll admit Eva seems a lot happier the last few days, but I'm pretty sure it's going to take a lot more than a month sober for her to get anywhere near as blissed out as this lady.

Her name is Val and she's been clean and sober seven years. She's the speaker tonight so she's standing up there behind a lectern telling this giant room of people about all of the crazy things she's done. She says having an addiction is the same as having a mental illness and these meetings are her medicine. She says all the people in these rooms are her doctors. Then she starts pointing at people randomly, saying "You" to the old wheezing guy with the oxygen tank, "You" to the housewife in the matching pink sweater set, "You" to the Indian man with the long black braid and carved-up-looking face, and "You" to me, just a kid with a month sober and one night left in rehab, dreading going home to his delusional mother.

Me with my fear and confusion and secrets. Me with my sad excuse for a life. The most living I've ever done has been in this last month, and I've been locked up in rehab. How could I possibly help someone like her? How does that make any kind of sense?

Val used to have sex with men for drugs. She's up there telling us all about it, and she's *laughing*, and people in the audience are *laughing*, and I guess I must have missed something, because where I come from it's not funny to have sex with men for drugs. She's talking about it like it's the most natural thing in the world, and people in the audience are nodding their heads like it's the most natural thing in the world, and she's like, "It's amazing what we do to get high, isn't it?" and someone's like "Amen, sister," and she's like, "Really, it made total sense at the time," and everyone's like, "Ha, ha, ha," and I don't know if I'll ever get to the point where I can laugh about the things I've done, but it sure seems like it feels a lot better than the way I have been feeling, and maybe if I stick around long enough and keep listening to people like Val, maybe then I'll figure out what's so funny and I can start laughing like everybody else instead of feeling like such crap all the time.

How can she stand up there so tall as she's telling us how her mother beat her and her father molested her when she was a little girl? How is it possible for her to look so proud? How is she not being consumed by shame? She should be disintegrating before our eyes. She should be struck by lightning, and God's big, angry, booming voice should be shaking the room with "How dare you? I told you never to tell." But that's not her God, she says. Her God is loving and kind and wants what's best for her. Her God loves peace and serenity and forgiveness. Her God doesn't make her keep secrets. I thought I knew God all my life, but maybe it was some other guy the whole time. I want this God. I want Val's God. I want a God who doesn't make me jump through hoops and hate myself to earn his love.

I kind of wish Eva was sitting next to me, it being our last night here and all, but I understand she has to spend as much time with her beloved New Guy before she graduates tomorrow. Besides, she only lives a few miles away from me, and Shirley convinced my mom it'll be good for me to nurture the relationships I've made in treatment. I'm going over to her house for dinner the day after tomorrow, so it's not like we're never going to see each other again. Her dad's going to make tacos. Then we're all going to watch a movie together, which Eva thinks is weird, but I think it's kind of nice. She says it's too late for him to start acting like a parent, but I know she's secretly happy about it. I'm trying not to think too much about my mom and how she's determined to stay exactly the same. I could sit here feeling sorry for myself, but I figure, what's the point? There's not a whole lot I can do about it. Serenity comes from accepting the things I cannot change, right? I bet Shirley would be proud of me for this mature thinking.

Val's up there glowing and confident, and I wonder if I can ever be anywhere near as strong as her someday. She says she can forgive her parents today, and I don't want to say she's lying, but I really do not understand how that's possible. She also says she's gay and she doesn't have to hate herself for it anymore. I look around and wait for someone to say something, to snicker, to roll their eyes, to elbow the person sitting next to them, but nothing like that happens. It's just the same nodding heads and serene faces, supporting her and taking it all in.

She ends her speech, and everyone claps, and people raise their hands for the next half hour to thank her and share three-minute versions of their thoughts and feelings. I take the meeting schedule out of my pocket that I picked up on the way in, and I circle the entry for this meeting. There's a meeting at this church four days out of the week, and my house is just a short walk away. I'm sure my mom won't be thrilled about me spending so much time in an Episcopalian church (full of homosexuals, abortionists, and communists, according to her), but that's not really any of her business, is it? She can't keep me locked inside the house, and let's be honest—it's not like she can chase after me.

Everyone gets up and holds hands, and I can tell that Eva's crying and trying to hide it because she keeps wiping her eyes with her sleeve. The AC with us tonight is some new guy, and all the patients are new, so no one even realizes what a big deal tonight is. Don't they know Eva and I are going home tomorrow? Don't they know what that means?

And then it hits me. I'm going home tomorrow. All of a sudden I'm terrified. All of a sudden I don't think I can breathe. All of a sudden that cheesy thing people say jumps into my head—"Today is the first day of the rest of your life"—and I know nothing will ever be the same again.

Val starts walking my way, shaking hands and giving hugs

to everyone along the way. She catches my eye and smiles. She keeps getting closer, and even though I want to, I don't run away. I can't. It's like I'm frozen.

"Hi," she says when she reaches me. "I'm Val. You with the rehab?"

"Uh-huh," is what I think I say.

"Lucky kid. I wish someone put me in rehab when I was your age."

All I can do is nod my head. I'm using all my strength to keep from freaking out.

"You look tense," she says.

"I'm getting out tomorrow," I tell her. I don't know where it comes from. Why am I telling this to a total stranger?

"That's big," she says. "How are you feeling?"

"I'm scared," I tell her.

"I know," she says.

"I don't know what to do," I tell her.

"Of course you don't," she says, and for some reason I keep talking, waiting for her to stop me, waiting for her to either tell me to shut up or give me some profound insight that makes everything clear. But all she does is stand there and listen as I explode my fears and insecurities all over. All she does is let me speak until I've run out of things to say. Then she puts her hand on my shoulder and squeezes. "Did that feel good?"

"I don't know," I say. "I don't know anything."

"Well, I have some good news."

"What?"

"It gets better," she says. "I swear."

"But what if it doesn't?"

"It does."

"But what if it doesn't?"

She squeezes my shoulder again. "Didn't you just say you don't know anything?"

"I guess."

"So why are you trying to act like you know everything?"

"I don't know."

She starts fishing around in her bag. She pulls out a pen and a scrap of paper and starts writing.

"Here's my number," she says, handing me the piece of paper. "You're going to call me as soon as you get home tomorrow."

"Really?"

"Yes."

"What if you're busy?"

"I'll call you back," she says. "They have this thing called voice mail these days. Have you heard of it?" It takes me a second to realize she's making a joke. "And guess what?" she says.

"What?"

"You have homework tonight. Are you ready? First assignment: For fifteen minutes you have to write down everything you're grateful for."

"Everything?"

"Let's practice. Think fast. Name three things you're grateful for. Go."

"Um, I don't know," I say. I panic. "My hair?"

"Your *hair*? Are you kidding me? What else?"

"I don't know."

"How about your sobriety?"

"Um, yes?"

"All right," she says. "We have some work to do." That's when Eva comes up and hooks her arm through mine and tells me it's time to go.

"This is my friend Eva," I tell Val.

"Well, she's lucky to have you," Val says, and Eva smiles, and I can't help but smile too. Val wants me to call her tomorrow, and Eva's my best friend, and I guess this is the first time I've ever really been able to call someone that, and I don't know, it just feels good. Like maybe I'm not so alone anymore. Like maybe I have someone to talk to when I feel like I'm the only person in the world.

"Bye," I say, and start walking toward where the AC and the other kids are waiting for us.

"Hey, hold on a sec," Val says. I turn around, and she's standing there with her arms spread wide, and I guess that means I'm supposed to hug her. I let her put her arms around me, and I'm surprised that it doesn't feel weird, just warm and safe and smelling kind of like cinnamon. "Hey," she says. "I have one more thing for you to feel grateful for."

"What?"

"You don't ever have to get fucked up again."

I smile and take a deep breath. It's true. I never have to get fucked up again. And that's the best news I've heard in a long time.

OLIVIA

Hi, guys!

I don't know if this letter is going to get to you in time. Maybe you've all gone home already. I really wanted to write to you as a group, but I'm probably too late. Dad was going to ask Shirley if she would send everyone a copy of this letter, so I guess that's better than nothing.

I'm sad that I didn't get to say good-bye. It's like I was with you one day, then all of a sudden I wasn't, and now I don't know if I'll ever see any of you again. I try not to think about that. I try to pretend like I'll just run into everyone at lunch, then it'll be time for Group and we'll all complain like we always do even though we secretly look forward to it. It's weird being in this hospital with all these doctors and nurses who don't know anything about me except what it says in my chart. It feels like I was just plucked out of my real life and placed in a hospital TV drama, and I'm an actor playing the "poor anorexic drug-addict girl." Except it's way more boring than anything you'd see on TV, and the doctors aren't anywhere near as cute.

Mostly what I wanted to tell you is that I'm okay. And I'm sorry for scaring you. I don't really remember anything, but the doctors told me it probably looked a lot like it does in the movies, with all the shaking and eyes rolling back in my head, plus I bit my tongue, so the blood probably freaked you out. When blood starts coming out of a person's mouth in movies, it usually means they're a goner. But don't worry, it wasn't anything a couple stitches couldn't fix.

I'm leaving for a new treatment center tomorrow, and I'll be there for at least three months. This one's in sunny San Diego, and the brochure shows happy girls walking on the beach with a pink sunset behind them. Who knows? Maybe I'll start surfing. (In case you couldn't tell, that was my lame attempt at a joke.) This place specializes in dual diagnoses of eating disorders and addictions, and they have a specially trained medical staff on-site all the time. I'm feeling really hopeful about it, like maybe I actually have a chance to get better. To be happy. It's funny, I just realized that my whole life, the whole time I've been trying to be perfect, I never once considered *happiness* as part of the equation. I guess it seemed so impossible I couldn't even let myself fantasize about it. But now, I don't know, things feel different somehow. Like impossible things might not be so impossible. Maybe that just means my antidepressants are working. (That was another joke, by the way.)

So Shirley ended up telling my dad and the doctors about my mom. Apparently doctor-patient confidentiality doesn't count if they think someone's life is in danger. But don't worry, Shirley, I'm not mad at you. Actually, it's a relief to have everything out in the open. I got so used to carrying secrets around, I didn't realize how heavy they are. It was literally killing me. I wish I had been brave enough to tell my dad the truth, and it wouldn't have taken something like this to happen for everyone to start being honest. I guess I was afraid no one would believe me. Or worse, they wouldn't care. Like believing me would cause too much trouble and it'd be easier for everyone to just keep pretending nothing was wrong.

But that's not what happened at all. People can surprise you, I guess. Dad doesn't want to give me all the "unfortunate details" as he calls them, but I do know that my mom is currently staying at her family's estate in North Carolina instead of living in our house. At first I was worried about my little brother, but to be honest, the nanny and the maid are his real mothers and always have been. Dad won't tell me if they're getting a divorce, because he says I don't need to worry about that right now, but I know he's been talking to his lawyers because they keep calling and he has to "step out for a minute." You'd think I'd be upset, or maybe even happy, but honestly I don't feel anything. I don't think I've thought of her as my mother for a long time. I guess if I feel anything, it's relief. I'm sure there's something deeper going on, and I'll be in therapy about it soon enough, but for right now I just don't want to think about it. I know that's probably bad and Shirley would say I'm in denial or something, but seriously—I can only deal with so much at a time. Being in a hospital because I had an anorexic seizure is enough for right now.

My dad's been here with me this whole time. I think this is probably the most time I've spent with him my whole life. I can tell he feels bad about it, because it's like he's trying to make up for it every way he can, like trying to be extra nice and attentive. But mostly we just play cards a lot. I think he's letting me win. I've told him about you guys, and he thinks you're all great (but Jason's a bit of a smart-ass—sorry, Jason). He's going to help me move to the new treatment center. Then I guess I'm on my own again for a while.

I know I should say something hopeful and positive about starting this new chapter in my life or whatever, and I am hopeful, but the truth is I'm also really scared. What if I'm too screwed up to fix? Even when I was with you guys, even though I really wanted to get better, I still couldn't eat, even though I knew it was the right thing to do. I guess I can't expect you guys to understand, but it's like an addiction, only instead of drugs, I'm addicted to not eating. Well, I guess I'm addicted to both, really. God, I'm a mess. What if I'm so broken I can never do something as basic as feed myself? Do you realize how twisted that is? It amazes me sometimes that humans still exist. We're just animals, after all. And how can an animal get so removed from nature that it loses the instinct to keep itself alive? Really, we should be extinct. Or at least I should.

I've been alone my whole life, but for some reason I'm really scared to be alone now. I'm scared to be without you guys. You all saved my life. You know that? I don't know how to explain it quite right (and of course you know I've tried because this is probably the fiftieth draft of this letter). It's like I used to be alone and I didn't even care. I could have died and it didn't really matter. But something about knowing you, something about you seeing me and paying attention to how I was feeling and what I was thinking, something about mattering to you—it made me start thinking that maybe I cared what happened to me too. And what if that doesn't happen at the new place? I'm afraid the girls there won't be anything like you. I'm afraid our friendships will drift away and we'll lose touch and it'll be like we never even met. But how can we forget each other after everything we've gone through together? It's like we're a permanent part of each other, even if we never see each other again. No matter what happens, we're forever connected by this piece of our lives, this month we were forced together and shown things about ourselves we can never forget no matter how hard we try.

Shirley always talked about how important it is to be assertive about what you need, so here goes—I'd really like it if you'd write me letters (the old-fashioned kind with stamps because they don't have Internet where I'm going). I know you're all probably settling back into your normal lives, and you're busy, but I hope you can just take a minute to tell me how you're doing. Because I care about you and I want to know you're okay. This is kind of embarrassing, but you're the first friends I've ever really had, which is pretty sad, since you all probably hated me most of the time. But I want you to know that even when I was being a total bitch and not talking to anyone, I was still paying attention, and I was grateful for you the whole time. I haven't had a lot of practice having friends, but I want you to know that I liked you all the moment I met you, and even if we lose touch, I'm pretty sure I'll consider you my friends for the rest of my life.

Well, that's about it. If I write any more, I'll probably start crying, and I'm so tired of doing that. I hope you take care of yourselves and stay sober, because you deserve it. You really do. You deserve everything you want in life. Even if it's hard to believe sometimes, even if you think

you're not good enough or you've screwed up
too bad to deserve anything good, I know in my
heart you deserve to be happy. I really do.
Because you're the best people I've ever
known.

Love always,
Olivia

ACKNOWLEDGMENTS

For my agent, Amy Tipton, who continues to astound me with her strength and brilliance. This book would have been nothing without you.

For my editor, Anica Rissi, for always knowing the exact right thing to say. And for making me a mix CD of Weird Al Yankovic songs.

For my friend Kate Gagnon, for being such a gifted editor that she didn't even have to read the manuscript to know how to help me figure out the ending.

For my husband, Brian Relph, for being my biggest fan, my best friend, and my home.

For Peanut the Wonder Dog, even though you don't know how to read.

For Chandra, my Monday-night girls and bois, and the rest of my extended acronym family. You taught me what strength is. You loved me back to life.